MUDDVILLIANS

BY DRU DRU

This is a work of fiction. Names, characters, places, and incidents either are the products of the author's imagination or are used fictitiously. Any resemblance to actual persons, living or dead, businesses, companies, events, or locales is entirely coincidental.

Disclaimer: The publisher is providing this book and its contents on an "as is" basis and make no representations or warranties of any kind with respect to this book or its contents. In addition, the publisher assumes no responsibility for errors, inaccuracies, omissions, or any other inconsistencies herein.

Table of Contents

Dedication

This book is dedicated to the streets. 139th and Grace. For all the pain I've caused and all the destruction I was a part of. I will never be able to pay the debt that I owe but this book is the beginning of me trying.

PROLOGUE

To the outside world, (media, police, politicians, prosecutors, judges) those who don't understand some who don't even care to understand he was just another thug who caught some slugs. No big deal. But to the citizens of Muddville (Robbins, ILLINOIS-139th and Grace Street aka The Old Projects) it was a big deal. To them he wasn't just a number he was one of them. He walked like them, talked like them and born with his back against the wall shorty fought like them.

O.G.'S in the hood looked at him and saw themselves. Someone they wished they could have as a son or at the very least they wished their sons could be a little like him. Born in a different place at a different time he could have grown to be something great, with the right guidance maybe the second Black President.

However, he was born and raised in one of if not the suburb of the southside of Chicago, where the odds of being a victim of the streets was greater than graduating eighth grade. This is his story... I hope you can relate if not just try to understand because this story is for you.

Let's Take a Trip

The sky was gray, dark gray; The thunder was deafening; The raindrops were the size of grapes; Everybody visiting the Burr Oak Cemetery was soaking wet. None of it affected Isis as she mourned the one-year anniversary of her son's death.

Her son didn't just pass away peacefully, no her son was brutally murdered. He was shot six times. Those six shots are the reasons why she finds herself soaking wet at the Burr Oak Cemetery mourning, instead of celebrating his sixteenth birthdate, (You got this right his birthday was his death date) he would have been sixteen.

The thought bought water to Isis eyes though she blinked back the tears. She wouldn't let herself cry today. The saddest part of her son's death wasn't the way he was killed, it's the person who killed. Isis body began to shake at the thought. That's how hard it was to fight back her tears.

Shaun intertwined his arm with Isis to assure her she wasn't alone. Shaun didn't know what she was thinking but he had an idea. Shaun's gesture comforted Isis, it also her realize that she wasn't the only one in mourning, there were others who came to pay respects to her son.

1

Friends or associates or "the guys" as he used to say. She could hear him now; "Ma stop tripping these the folks." At one time those words use to make her laugh, not so much anymore.

"I can't believe it's been a year already." Tanisha sniffled.

The pain Isis felt paled into comparison to what Tanisha felt, life had cheated Tanisha.

"He was such a good kid." Ms. Loraine spoke.

She had watched both Isis and her son grow up in the projects, everybody called her granny even her own kids. There was no doubt granny would miss her son, Isis knew. Sure, Granny would find someone else to run her errands, take out he trash every morning, make sure her grass was cut because everyone loved her little garden outside the little project buildings.

She would even be able to have someone to go into her attic to get the Christmas tree. Nobody would say no to granny, not a crack dealer or a crack smoker. The thing is with her son Granny didn't have to ask. The thought put a smile on Isis tear-stained face.

A mixture of teenagers, young men and older men approached the tombstone but not before acknowledging Isis who knew them all. She

2

either grew up with them; watched them grow up or they watched her grow up. All of them were hurt, the grief was all over their faces. Isis stepped back to give them their space to mourn, Shaun and Tanisha followed suit. Shaun on her left Tanisha on he right, they were her crutches.

Isis watched on in amazement as they reminisced with her son as if he were there in the flesh on the good, bad, and ugly times. "Fucked up you got us pouring henn already." Isis heard but couldn't make out who spoke the words. They all took a sip and blessed the bottle one last time, by tapping it with pitchforks before emptying the rest onto the gravesite.

Shaun felt Isis tense up. "It's okay, it's just there way of sending love." He whispered in her ear while rubbing her back which was enough to calm her, but she still didn't agree with it even if it came with the lifestyle her son adopted or rather it adopted her son.

Thunder shook the cemetery followed by a sharp lightning that split the gray sky allowing the sun to shine bright. Isis could only smile, she could her him now. "Ma stop tripping on the guys." She knew he was also telling her everything would be okay. He was still watching over her, being his mother's protector that's all he wanted to be Isis told herself she wouldn't do it because it was too painful but somehow, she found

herself taking a trip down memory lane.

Poor Isis, that's his mommas name

Isis entered the Robbins Police Station strutting to the front desk as if on a runway and she was Tyra Banks in her prime. The look on the officer's face behind the glass was that of a deer caught in headlights. Isis was used to those types of looks by now.

"Hello. I'm Isis. I'm here to pick up my son."

Isis did her best to hide her true feelings because she was beyond pissed and this officer wasn't making it any better. If he was going to stare at least he could do his job while doing so.

"Sure. I'm gonna have to see some I.D."

"Of course." Isis had to fight with herself not to roll her eyes as she slid her state I.D. along with her son's birth certificate under the window.

The officer didn't need Isis identification in fact they wanted to get the boy out of their hair as soon as possible. At twelve years old there wasn't much they could do with him, but his time would come. They already placed ten to one bet that in the next few years he would be in a box they just didn't know whether to bet on that box being a jail cell or a casket.

This officer only wanted more time to admire the beautiful woman before him. If he had to guess her age, he'd say twenty-four and maybe stretch it to twenty-six. But she had the eyes of a forty-year-old which let the officer know she seen a lot. His eyes traveled her body for any signs of imperfections or the slightest sign of motherhood, they found none.

Her 34-D cup breast stood nice and firm holding their own with no bra support. There was no sign of stretch marks on the hint of cleavage she revealed. Her stomach was flat with no signs of excess weight on top of a small waist, wide hips, and thick thighs that let him know Isis looked better from the back.

She was perfect and if it were up to him her face would be next to the word in every dictionary, add that to her five-foot ten-inch frame which was well over six feet at the moment thanks to the three-inch Roberto Cavalli's, Shoulder length dreads and voluptuous eyes Isis could pass for an Egyptian goddess. Osiris himself wouldn't object to that.

Isis knew she looked good; she'd become numb to the stares she received from both men and women. Her five-ten one hundred- and fifty-five-pound frame demanded attention, it's also what paid the bills but now she wasn't in the mood.

"Is that all sir?" Isis had taken the officer out of his lustful fantasy.

"Ye...Ye... Yes ma'am... ummm... Detective Jones is expecting you." Not one time did the officer look over the information Isis had given him.

The officer watched as Isis walked away, hypnotized by the sway of her hips, unconsciously biting a hole in his bottom lip.

"Sorry, something just came up. I'll have to get back to you."

Detective Jones was in the middle of an important phone call when Isis entered his office knocking.

"If that call was important, I could have waited." Isis said as she took a seat across from Jones desk crossing her right leg over her left all the while smiling because she enjoyed the power, she held over heartless men like Detective Jones who only thought with their small head.

"No, it was nothing really." Jones lied. "Now how may I help you."

If Isis wasn't mistaking, he was referring to the Pot of gold resting between her thighs because that's where his eyes were focused.

"Excuse me." Isis was almost a hundred percent sure what he meant.

"I mean what brings you to my office."

Jones was now playing the same games as the officer behind the glass window. He knew exactly why she was there.

"I'm here to get my son out of that rat hole in the back you call a jail cell." Even though the smile never left her face there was no mistaken how serious Isis was.

Jones leaned back in his seat with his pointer finger against his nose as if in deep thought. He snapped his fingers as if he finally got it.

"Yeah. Of course, you mean the robber."

Isis was no longer smiling.

"Robber. I don't understand."

Detective Jones went on to explain he was leaving Crissy's snack shop with a corn beef and a fruit Punch Guzzler when he heard "this is a robbery. If you give me your money you want, get hurt." Jones wouldn't hesitate to pull the trigger. However, Jones realized that it was only a BB gun and knocked it away and within three seconds he was handcuffed. Being that Jones was wearing plain clothes he had no idea he was robbing a policeman.

"Oh my god. I am so sorry."

"Don't worry about it. Trust me this is nothing the cook county juvenile center can't fix."

Those words gave Isis an instant headache she knew CCJDC otherwise known as the Audi home was no place for her baby. Being home to the worse juvenile offenders in the country it would eat him alive.

"Is there anything I could do, anyth ng? Just please don't send my baby to that horrible place." Isis begged and pleaded.

"Sorry but it's out of my hands." Jones lied playing on her vulnerability. He hadn't even filed a incident report let along thought about charges.

Isis got up to close the door. There was no way she was letting her son go to jail.

"Are you sure there's nothing you could do?" Isis had made her way behind the detectives des, she was now standing between his legs.

He looked at the black beauty eyes filled with infatuation more so than lust, throat too dry to speak but the small bulge in his jeans let Isis know she had him. She unloosened the belt that held her leather jacket closed revealing her D-cups. Instinctively Jones reached out to feel them and she let him for a short second before stepping away. The tables had turned, and Isis was in control. Isis picked up the phone and handed it to detective Jones. "Make the call" she ordered, and he did. Isis straddled his lap her hot box on top of his erection her breast in his face and began to grind. Jones went to bite on her nipple, but she pushed his head away. He tried to palm her ass, but she removed his hands,

"Enjoy but don't touch."

She grinded harder the feeling caused Jones eyes to roll and eventually brought him to climax. To Isis it was a small price to pay.

Momma ain't strong enough to raise no boy

"Boy let this damn brown go." Isis seethed through gritted teeth as she literally fought her only son for control.

Initially she started out with a belt but no matter how hard she swung it he showed no sign of pain which is why she moved on to the broomstick, but he wouldn't let her use it.

"No ma, please don't hit me with this broom." He pleaded but at the same time he said it with force.

Isis couldn't believe her ears. Somebody had to be losing their mind. Whether it was him or her she didn't know.

Boy let this damn broom go." Isis snapped smacking him so hard the entire left side of his face turned red.

He still held on to the broom. "Sorry ma, but you not hitting me with this broom." He was serious.

Isis could see it in his twelve-year-old eyes, and it finally set in that she was losing her heart, her soul, her son. Refusing to accept this reality Isis mastered all her strength and yanked the broom away and ended up tripping over her Robert Cavalli. Before she hit the ground, he was right there by her side tears threatening to fall from his eyes. He was now her baby boy again.

"I'm so sorry ma. Are you alright?"

Even the thought of his mother being hurt pained him. Helping her up he led Isis to his bed. The roles had switched he was now the caregiver.

"Lay down ma, I'll get you something to drink."

"No baby sit down we need to talk."

Even though he didn't want to talk he obeyed his mother. "What's wrong ma?"

He stared into her light brown eyes as she stared into his hazels in return. The love and core he had for her was evident but what she couldn't see in those beautiful eyes was her twelve-year-old baby, instead she saw his father who with his shoulder length braids and a few freckles spread throughout his face, he was the spitting image of. Isis was looking at a young man.

"Baby why are you trying to drive your mother crazy?" Isis smoothed her hand down his designer braids.

"Ma I just want to take care of you that's all." He laid his head on her chest something she'd hoped he'd never grow out of.

His words stung her but the look in his eyes as he spoke to them, pained her because they let her know he wase dead serious. But he was only a child and that's all his mother needec him to be.

"Baby mommy doesn't need anything." Isis wrapped her arms around him while placing her cheek on top of his head, "Let momma do her job and take care of you."

Their project apartment had three bedrooms two of which belonged to him, one for him to sleep in the other a game room with all the latest games. Anything a kid could want was in that room. The kids in the projects always asked Isis if they could go up and play. Isis rarely said no because she knew how it felt to go without.

In the back he had a little motorcycle, mini dirt bike, mini four-wheeler, and a go-cart. The projects helped themselves to those as well. They had so much love and respect even the crackheads didn't steal from them. Why steal from someone who'd give you their last? His closet put grown men to shame as it was filled with Ralph Lauren, Pelle Pelle, Auou, True Religion, and 8732. If it was hot, he had it.

His shoe game was simple Mikes and Airforce one's all white low tops unless some special ones came out that he liked. He also rocked the Havana Joes from time to time everybody had to have at least one pair of Joes, but his favorites were the Aidi zero's and 773' by Derrick Rose. Isis didn't like the shoes, but he would say "Ma, that's the big homie." "You don't even know him." Isis responded, "So what that's one of the guys." And Isis would relent.

In fear of her son becoming a target she kept his jewelry simple both of his ears were pierced; he had a custom-made necklace the charm had love going down and mom going across but instead was a small picture of him and Isis. He'd lost count of the number of G-Shock watches, but he had one to match whatever he decided to wear. When it came to the love of her life Isis spared no expense.

Isis always had a hard time getting him to dress up he always claimed he didn't want people to be jealous of him. The truth was he didn't see the guys in the projects with Gucci loafers, Versace sweaters, Stacy Adams or head to toe Louis Vuitton. If only he knew they were a dope boys dream.

When Isis was pregnant, she had hit rock bottom mentally and emotionally. The life inside of her felt everything she felt. That's why his sole purpose on earth what to protect her from harm. That's why he felt obligated to take care of her. The problem was that growing up in the projects he only knew two ways to do that. Sell dope or rob and the robbing way didn't work.

"But ma look what you have to do to take care of me."

That statement knocked the air out of Isis. She wouldn't have seen it coming a mile away.

"Sweety what is it that you think mommy does." Isis was all ears she needed to hear what her son had to say. She made it her business to keep her work away from him.

"I don't know ma" he didn't want to say it. "It's just that people talk and sometimes I don't like what I hear."

Isis should have known. The people who her son was referring to were none other than the females in the project's hating on hers because they couldn't get their own. But was it really Isis fault that they give it up for a pair of reeboks and a happy meal or was it theirs? They had no idea what Isis did for a living. They only knew that they saw her come from nothing to something. Haters..... Couldn't live with them but you damn sure couldn't live without them..... Their everywhere.

If they only knew Isis had hadn't had sex since the day she was impregnated. After what shed gone through Isis would never let another man between her legs or into her heart. But she didn't mind them calling her a hoe as long as they called her a paid hoe. However, Isis was a dancer, and she was in high demand. The offers Isis received from men to have sex would make a nun give it up, but every time Isis turned down a offer her demand went higher. Her clientele was the top if the food chain high priced lawyers, Fortune 500 CEO's million-dollar heirs.

"Trust me sweety none of those…" Isis had to catch herself from saying hoes. "People know what they are talking about."

Isis knew she was running late but didn't know how late until she check her frank Mueller, a gift from the client she's supposed to see tonight.

"Baby mommy has to…"

"No Mommy please." He whined before she finished her sentence. He hugged his mother tightly. He didn't want her to go. His whine cut through her soul and if she wouldn't have been paid in advance Isis wouldn't go.

"Baby. I have to go. I'll be back in a few hours. We can finish talking when you get back from school."

No words could explain how he felt at that moment as he watched his mother leave in a leather Jacket and heels. There was no secret what she was about to do. Even worse he knew she was doing it for him. He cried himself to sleep.

What's his father's name? Shorty never knew him

The next morning in school he couldn't focus. Isis didn't come home last night, and he was beyond worried. Everyone including the teacher noticed his sour mood. Normally he was the life of the classroom. During testing he kept everybody focused, during free time he kept everyone laughing. He talked to everyone the cool kids and the kids who didn't think they fit in with anyone.

He was never afraid to raise his hand and ask a question. Unlike other kids he wasn't embarrassed to be wrong as long as it was explained to him how he was wrong. He was every teachers dream; respectful, turned in work on time, worked well with others, these are just a few of the comments made on his report cards, in which he never brought home less than a B.

Tanisha didn't believe it when he told her he'd never studied a day in his life. She'd seen firsthand how smart he was that was impossible without studying. He was just a fast learner wise beyond his years with the humility to match. He was in the middle of his third period English 1 language arts class when his anxiety begins to get the best of him. He tapped Tanisha to get her attention.

"I'm about to leave." He mouthed.

"Leave....why?" She mouthed back.

"Isis didn't come home last night." Tanisha didn't respond her eyes were in disbelief. "Don't worry I'll be back to walk home with you." He knew that was on her mind. "They'd walk home together since head start. "Mr. C I need to use the bathroom."

Recognizing the voice Mr. c excused him without looking up. The bathroom was the last thing on his mind.

~~~~~~~~

One thing about the projects is nothing ever changed. No matter if it was two o'clock in the evening you got the same thing. Dope boys running up to cars so fast Usain bolt didn't stand a chance. O.G.'s chilling in the cut between two buildings everything going on the set. Further down toward the middle of the projects in front of the cigarette ladies building there was a nice size dice game.

A few females were spectating the dice game some were laughing and giggling.

"What's funny?" He asked.

Obviously, it was an inside joke because no one else paid them any mind.

"You are too little when you get older, you'll see."

He had known Keisha his entire life. She was light skinned and thick as mud. The thigs he heard about her he'd always wonder if they were true.

"Lil nigga why the fuck you ain't in school?"

He knew that voice from anywhere it was his best friend or more like his baby brother baby Ty. They weren't blood but they could pass for real brothers. Sometimes he wondered if baby Ty got that memo because sometimes, he would act like his daddy.

"I ain't on shit, I'm going home." He answered eyeing the hand full of money in baby Ty's hand. Obviously, the dice were good to him. He could have asked Baby Ty the same thing, but it would have probably led baby Ty into following him home just to kick his ass. So, he thought better of it and kept it moving or at least tried to.

"Hold on lil nigga... since yo lil bad ass ain't in school come hoot dice for me."

He couldn't deny the O.G. Red. The O.G demanded respect.

"But O.G I ain't never shot dice before." Unless playing dice with baby Ty and Tanisha counted, he was telling the truth.

"Just shake and roll, I'll take care of the rest." O.G made it simple. "I got twenty lil folks hit." Everybody jumped on the hit except baby Ty who rode with him. "Roll the dice lil G."

He did so and they came three one.

"I got twenty more he ten or four."

Everybody jumped on that ten four bet thinking he had too much pressure on him. It was nothing for O.G red to cover every bet, rumor was that O.G red money ran longer than Halsted and Halsted didn't stop. Unlike baby Ty who just had a hand full of money a second ago now stood with his hands in his pocket. He'd bet his last on the ten four bet. He rolled the dice again and they came the same way three one.

"That's what the fuck I'm talking about. Right back ain't no cheating." O.G. was geeked. "I got whatever lil folks hit again."

This time nobody got out their body. He looked at his brother from another who now had to hold all his money inside of his shirt and winked at him. Baby Ty nodded back and smirked. He knew his brother too well. That smirk meant he still had an ass whooping coming. So, he decided to leave while he was ahead before baby Ty got any ideas.

"Girl his momma gone kick his ass once she finds out he ditched school to shoot dice." Keisha said to her rat pack.

"Who his momma is?" Nikki wasn't even from the projects she just came digging for gold.

"You know that black bitch that always have her nose turned up. She drives the Audi A7." Keisha did her best to explain.

"Oh, the stripper? I ain't even know she had kids. I don't know how she pushed his yellow butt out that black ass."

Every word stung him like a bumble bee as he continued to walk home.

"What's his father name?" Nikki asked.

He continued to listen because he wanted to know the answer too.

"Both of you hoes need to shut the fuck up." Baby Ty came to Isis defense.

But he wasn't surprised by that, its why he called him brother.

O.G red ignored the rat pack his attention was on him walking home. O.G knew if the streets didn't claim him first, he'd grow to do amazing things.

Though he had his blood in him

He was so happy to see his mother's Audi parked in the alley he couldn't help himself as he took off in full out sprint. He wanted no he needed to feel her warm embrace now more than ever. Everything he heard the rat pack say about Isis only made him love her more because whatever it was that his mother did, she did it for him.

Using the key, he let himself in so fast he almost fell running up the stairs trying to get to Isis. To his dismay she wasn't in her room. After checking both rooms along with the bathroom, he backtracked downstairs to the living room, kitchen, and utility room there was still no Isis. He started to panic, heart racing, body sweating. Something wasn't right, then the thought came to check her car. As he jogged toward the Audi, he could already see that Isis wasn't inside, but he still put his face against the glass anyway. He felt helpless all he could do was sit on the hood with his head in his hands.

"I swear to God you gone make me kill you one of these days."

His ears parked at the sound of her voice.

"Why the hell aren't you in school?"

Even upset her voice was music to his ears he instantly felt joy inside. Followed by jealously as he watched Isis step out of the car with another man. A man he didn't know. He was the only man worthy of his mother's presence. Then he felt anger as the two approached him side by side as if they known each other for years.

"Boy why did you leave school?"

He heard her loud and clear, but his attention was on the man in front of him, searching his face for any signs of familiarity it was a habit. This face did look familiar, but he knew it wasn't the face he was looking for. He didn't even know what face he was looking for. He just hoped to find it one day.

"Ma who is this?" Not once did he take his eyes off the man in front of him.

"None of your business, why did you leave school?"

"I didn't see you before I left so I came back to make sure you were alright." He never took his eyes off the man in front of him.

Isis was upset but more with herself. He was getting worse by the day, and she felt helpless learning to be a mother on the fly. Only Lord knew what he'd do next.

"Ma who is this?" He asked again breaking her train of thought.

Like Isis once he got his mind wrapped around something there was no letting go so, she might as well get it over with.

"Baby this is Shaun we used to be good friends, but he left...moved away."

Believe none of what you hear but half of what you see but one plus one would always equal two no matter how you did the math. And the math said Isis was pregnant when he left the hood. But if he'd known Shaun would never have left her.

"Isis is this..."

"Yes...Yes..." She cut him off but the look in her eyes told Shaun all he needed to know. But he didn't need words. There was no denying whose blood was pumping through shorties veins.

Isis pressed the unlock button on her key ring, "Come on baby let mommy take you back to school." Her voice cracked as she spoke.

"No ma we're supposed to finish our talk remember?"

Isis felt a migraine coming on. What was she supposed to do he was becoming more rebellious by the day.

"Please ma I miss you." He buried his head in her chest, "I miss you ma."

He did really miss her but there was just something about this Shaun character that made his mother emotional. He wrapped his arms around her waist to ensure her that he was there for her. If only he knew that he was the source of her heartbreak. It wasn't her fault nor his it was just the hands they were dealt. On the outside looking in one would call him a mommas boy. Shaun believed that was the case. Shaun also knew that while Isis may have been the parent lil dude was the guardian. And that was a recipe for a disaster.

Hot temper, she say he act just like her husband

The message on Isis voicemail was clear. Until Isis showed up for an emergency conference her son would not be allowed back into the school. His education was something Isis wouldn't take to chance which is why she wasted no time going to Kellar Kellar school with her son in tow. You would have thought she was a lawyer the way she pleaded her sons case, but it still wasn't enough.

"I'm sorry but we have a zero-tolerance policy for your sons behavior. As much as I hate to do this, I'm going to have to suspend him for ten days with the possibility of expulsion."

"Expelled. For one infraction in three years."

"I understand he's not a troublemaker however, we have to set examples. Kids can't leave the school on their own accord."

He listened as his mother and Mr. Wilson went back forth. He didn't mind ten school free days until it really hit him.

"Mr. Wilson."

"Yes son."

His skin instantly turned red he hated when people called him that. Isis didn't even call him son.

"If you miss more than seven days, don't you automatically fail?"

"Yes." Mr. Wilson acknowledged.

Isis didn't speak in fear that what she had to say would make things worse. Her son had the best grade point average in the school. At best his actions warranted a three-day suspension but then she understood. Mr. Wilson was no different than detective Jones using her son as Pawn to get to her. That's why she hated niggas.

Isis couldn't stand to see her sons education go up in flames. He was only a kid the importance of an education hadn't registered with him yet. But it had with Isis. Life was hard enough with a education without one it was ten times worse. Hell, hood restaurants like momma Doos required a high school diploma.

Nobody told Isis it would be that way she learned from hands on experience forced to drop out of high school to take care of herself and the child she had on the way. Abandoned by her parents after her refusal to get an abortion. She'd die before she let her son travel down that same road of degradation.

"I'm sure we can work something out." Isis had softened her tone.

"I'm sorry but my hands are tied."

Isis was a hundred percent sure he caught her meaning he just wanted to be sure that's what she meant.

"Are you sure?" Isis made eye contact with him with her eyes she led his down to her 34 d's. Now, he was sure.

Mr. Wilson had wanted Isis from the moment he laid eyes on her almost three years ago as she registered her son for school. He didn't want to have sex with her, he wanted to taste her. He wanted to know if she tasted as good as she looked. Now was his opportunity. He had a hard on from the moment Isis stepped into his office. She wore a Christian Dior button down that teased him as it revealed the slightest bit of cleavage that jiggled a little with the slightest bit of movement. The matching vest just accentuated her breast even more Mr. Wilson drunk it all in all five foot ten inches of her. Isis was aware of the power she held over Mr. Wilsons type. She knew her sons education was safe.

"Ummm...maybe there is something we could do." The possibilities of a night with Isis had Mr. Wilson oozing pre cum. "Are you free at six?" Mr. Wilson was eyeing his mother like a juicy steak, and all was going through his mind were the things he heard. All the rumors about his mother. Then Mr. Wilson licked his lips and went off.

"Hell, naw she ain't free at six!"

He didn't see it coming he only felt the pain and tasted the blood from the black slap his mother delivered.

"Watch your damn mouth. Have you lost your mind?"

"I'm sorry ma." He sucked the blood. He knew he delivered it for disrespecting his mother. He just couldn't help it.

Mr. Wilson knew he'd never get this opportunity again he wasn't letting go that easy. Any other principal would be on the phone calling DCFS any other principal who was thinking with the right head.

"So, six o'clock good" His eyes were focused between her thighs as if could see through the Christian Dior slacks she wore. It was the straw that broke the camel's back.

"Stop staring at my momma like that."

He went into a rampage knocking everything off Mr. Wilsons desk starting with the computer. Mr. Wilson caught with his hand in the cookie jar could do nothing but watch. Isis just knew she was having a case of Déjà vu. It was like seeing his father all over again. He too would go into a rage if he felt another man was looking at Isis the wrong way for too long, that's one person who Isis didn't want her baby to become.

After there was nothing left to destroy Isis was able to calm him down. Mr. Wilson knew he had fucked up as he watched the two leave his office. Before driving away Isis looked at her son in the passenger seat looking cool as can be. One couldn't tell that he was just the Tasmanian Devil just minutes earlier. She shook her head in dread. He acted too much like him.

Before leaving for work Isis made it clear that he was not to leave not even to go to the candy store. But she was leaving and if he went out how would she know? With that knowledge he would disobey his mother for the first time. But in his mind, it was for the right reason. Isis always told him that people on the streets didn't know what they were talking about. But he was old enough to know with every lie told, the truth lay somewhere within.

What hurt the most was that he knew she was doing it all for him. She'd always taken good care all for him and now it was time for him to return the favor. He was going to make it to where Isis never had to entertain another man again. If only he knew... His mother had more than enough money already. In the beginning it was about the money but if that was till the case now, she could have quit years ago. After she secured his college tuition and trust fund that he'd receive once he turned twenty-five.

In fact, she did try to quit and that's when she realized it wasn't about the money it was about revenge. Revenge on Men like her father and her sons father. The only two men she'd ever loved abandoned her. She realized men didn't care about their responsibilities, rules, or expectations. The only thing they cared about was money, so that's where she hit them. In their pockets and most importantly she hit their egos. The looks in their eyes as she left them ten to twenty thousand dollars poorer.

The blow it gave them once it set in that they would never get to taste her goodness. It was all too addictive. And she wasn't doing it for herself she was doing it for women across the world who had to deal with the Bill Cosby and Roger Ailes types.

Daddy didn't fuck with him

Like most shorties growing up in the hood he thought he knew all he needed to know about the streets. It was in their faces in the morning when they walked to school. They saw it when they came home from school in the evening. They saw it on a normal day as they played in the projects as children do.

If a car drove through the projects, they could point out which one was coming to buy weed, which one was coming back to buy crack or which ones were just passing through. If a customer came through looking for a certain dealer, they knew which dealer the customer preferred. They even knew an unmarked police car when it came through. To them it was about to learn is that just like any other sport watching a game from the sideline was totally different from being in the field.

He thought he had it all figured out he just needed to be put on. Which isn't easy as many believe. Contrary to popular belief. Gang bangers, thugs, supe predators or whatever the label is today are not too quick to put shorties down. At least not those who upholds the chairman's vision which is and always be for us to be a positive productive person. A power to be reckoned with not in the streets but in boardrooms on the world stage. No one would wish this life on their worst enemy.

Those on the outside looking in who don't believe this who dot understand the struggle, look at Dwayne Wade and Derrick Rose. Listen to Stephen A. Smith on first take who'll never shy away from Hollis queens background and will let it be known that he was protected from the streets by those in the streets. Kendrick Lamar is a product of Compton he is where he is today because of those people in Compton. The list is long.

Baby Ty while only a couple years older was already knee deep in the game. He was fatherless with a crackhead for a mother leaving his grandmother to be their caretaker. The problem was she was very old and very sick. Therefore, the buck stopped with Baby Ty to take care of his grandmother and younger sister Tanisha. Like any man would he stepped up to the plate. Baby Ty was exactly where he knew he'd be, on the set trying to catch a customer.

"Baby Ty, What's good?" He said before getting too close. It was late and drug dealers didn't like surprises.

Baby Ty checked his Jo rodeo just in case he was tripping.

"Lil nigga shouldn't you be in the crib getting ready for school?"

The way Baby Ty looked at him he just knew he had a ass whooping coming.

"Man bro, I got kicked out over some bullshit."

"Hee Hee HaHa." Baby Ty did a phony laugh letting it be known he didn't believe him.

"Now get the fuck back in the house, you know Isis gone blame me."

"Bro Isis ain't home."

"Baby Ty let the sock response slide. It didn't matter If she was home or not. If she found out that was Baby Tys ass. He also knew there was a reason lil bro was out this late.

"Aight lil bro. What's up because right now there's only three types of people out? Crackheads, drug dealers, and stick-up kids. Make that four if you count the police." Baby Ty counted each one of his fingers for emphasis, "And you don't fit either one."

He began to have second thoughts, but it was now or never.

"I'm trying to jay down." He said softly avoiding Baby Ty's eyes by focusing his attention on a beer bottle that he didn't know was filled with piss until kicked it over.

Baby Ty began to laugh he thought it was because he'd gotten piss on the bottom of his. Akoo Jeans and all over six ring Mikes.

"Lil bro trying to get some ass. Wel , naw." Baby Ty continued to laugh but stopped once he realized his little brother was serious. "Somebody fucking with you or something, who is it?"

It was no secret that Baby Ty would go to war alone for his broski.

"No Baby Ty I'm trying to get money."

Baby Ty soften up.

"Damn bro why you ain't just say that? Got me ready to fuck a nigga up. How much you need?" Baby Ty pulled out his dope boy not.

He still didn't understand.

"No.... Tyshaun."

The only time he used Baby Ty's real name was when he was dead serious. Baby Ty knew this.

"I want to make my own money; I want to hustle."

Baby Ty instantly caught that feeling in his chest. It wasn't pain, it wasn't hurt but it was there, and he felt it. His little brother didn't know what he was asking for. If Baby Ty didn't have to sell drugs he wouldn't. Whoever say the streets was the easy way clearly wasn't talking about a hundred thirty ninth and Grace, but the survival of his family depended on him.

"Let's go play the game or something." Baby Ty didn't know what else to say he was lost.

But he saw through what Baby Ty was trying to do. It wouldn't work. Baby Ty realized that once lil bro handed him his house key.

"You could go but my mind is already made up. So, either show me the ropes or let me find out on my own."

Baby Ty was crying inside his brother has just made it very simple. His mind was made up and no matter what Baby Ty did it would be his fault was the lesser of two evils. Letting his brother jump into the Lion's den alone to be eaten alive which in some cases ended in death or he could protect him as much as possible. The answer was easy.

In the streets there was a saying, "The game is cold but its fair." Baby Ty accepted that saying as gospel until. Yes, the game was cold but there was nothing fair about what the streets were about to do to his thirteen-year-old brother. It was different from what they had done to some of the greats like Marcy, Franky J, Big Mike, or even B-nice. But the streets called and when the streets called, they demanded a answer.

In the hood keystone was arguably the most lucrative block when it came to the crack game. Keystone was right off a hundred thirty fifth, a hundred and thirty fifth street connected Robbins to three white Suburban towns; Midlothian, Crestwood, and Alsip. A dime bag in the projects went for twenty and sometimes fifty on Keystone. A few of the guys who weren't much older than Baby Ty told tales on how they used to sneak down to the fifth, hide in the cut and catch some of their customers. There was so much traffic the niggas down there didn't notice.

So he chose lesser of the two evils for Baby Ty because his little brother wouldn't be able to hustle in the projects. The guys wouldn't allow it. He had too much promise and no one would allow him to throw rocks at the penitentiary. So, the name of the game they were about to play was don't get caught because there was no secret that niggas on keystone didn't play.

That first night they didn't get caught in fact it went without any problems. The money was fast, and it was good, but they only stayed for two hours because neither knew when Isis would make it home. But they'd be back. They were grossed in a game of Madden NFL Football when Isis interrupted.

"Tyshaun, are you staying the night again?"

As always Isis used his real name something he wouldn't even allow his mother to do. Tyshaun's response got stuck in his throat as he stared up at Isis. From her perfect pedicured toes that were inside a pair of Chanel heels that wrapped around her tone calves from her ankles. Her matching skirt stopped just above her knee with a slit showing off just a touch of her chocolate thigh. The skirt fit her slim waist and curved hips perfectly. The same could be said for the blouse she wore. The only thing stopping her thirty-four D's from being exposed were two spaghetti straps, one around her neck the other around her mid back. She had the matching Chanel jacket folded on her arm.

"Stop staring at my momma like that fool." He smacked Baby Ty upside his head trying to get him back into the game, because Baby Ty had let the play clock run out.

"Are you staying tonight?" Isis asked again.

Still unable to speak Baby Ty nodded that he was.

"Okay don't forget about Tanisha." Isis placed her hand on her hip letting it be known how serious she was.

"Ma you know we ain't gone forget about that girl." He responded shaking his head.

Baby-Ty was still shaking his head for only God knew what. Baby-Ty was in love before now he always looked at Isis as his mother now, he was looking at her as a woman and like any other man he was smitten. Isis stepped in front of the T.V.

"Excuse me ma, you blocking the game."

Isis ignored his smartness she knew exactly what she was doing.

"Sweetie, I talked to the school again. As long as you makeup all of your work and stay out of trouble you'll be able to graduate on time."

"Okay ma, thank you." He was just ready for her to leave already.

At that point her mother's intuition kicked in. She couldn't put her finger on it, but something wasn't right. He could see the light go on in his mother's head. It meant she had gotten suspicious.

"I love you ma." He got up to kiss her on both cheeks. That's probably all she was waiting on.

"I love you too baby."

"Awww I'm jealous." Baby-Ty pouted.

"Boy, shut up and give me a hug."

Baby-Ty enjoyed every second every second of the hug. It felt like heaven and smelled like it also. If only he didn't have to let, go.

"Tyshaun what I tell about letting these girls play in your head."

Baby-Ty's dreads was twisted every way but the right way. He could only smile because the truth was, he used his dreads to get sex. These days every girl thought they could twist.

"Be where I could find you tomorrow." Isis said to Baby-Ty before leaving.

"You stupid." He saw after hearing the door close. They had lost valuable get money time.

"Bro yo moms is beautiful."

He waved Baby-Ty off. He didn't have time for it.

"Don't forget stupid that's your momma too."

"Fuck that I want her to be my wife."

Baby-Ty was irritating the fuck out of him.

"Whatever." He said as he began counting money. But Isis was still on Baby-Tys mind.

"Bro where she going?"

"Work." He said in disgust as he continued to count the money it took his mind off what Isis was going to do.

"Where she work at."

Baby-Ty knew damn well what was going on. He'd in multiple fights defending Isis name.

"Bro turns it down some." He said to Baby-Ty in all seriousness.

"You ever wonder what's up with your daddy."

They'd spoken about their fathers on numerous occasions. Baby-Ty was curious today because he wanted to put a face on the nigga dumb enough to leave Isis.

"Bro the nigga don't fuck with us like yours don't fuck with you. That's why we're brothers."

"You right to bro fuck them niggas, but you know what?" Baby-Ty smiled.

"What Tyshaun?" He was getting blew because he knew Baby-Ty was about to say something stupid as he was trying to count the money.

"When I marry Isis, you can call me daddy."

So, the streets raised him

The streets talk and when the streets talked, niggas listened. Therefore, it didn't take long for the hood to know he was hustling. Since he was already in the game it was his birthright to hustle in the projects. Many didn't like it, but it was his right. In his mind he owed a lot to Baby-Ty but in truth it was the other way around because of him Baby-Ty had become hood star at sixteen. It was the night they were at his house and his mother had left for work.

"Bro, we got over forty-five hundred dollars."

Neither could believe it. They'd only been hustling together for two weeks but they'd been saving everything using his shoe boxes for stash spots. No money was taken out unless it was for a necessity.

"Let's go cop a half ounce."

Baby-Ty was excited, but his mind was still on small scale.

"Man, bro I was thinking we spent it all on work."

The thought didn't sit well with Baby-Ty. Anything could happen. He saw it to.

"Turn that 62 to 125, 125 to a 250." He began.

"250 to a half a man ain't nothing nobody can do with me." Baby-Ty rhymed with him it was his favorite verse after all.

"Now who with me?" They both finished in unison. At that moment Baby-Ty finally understood what Jay meant. His mind was definitely on the right track. They copped their first nine piece.

Females had always been attracted to him but now it was different. He was always the freshest nigga wherever he went but now that everybody knew he was getting money he was now attracting females his mother's age. The mothers of the guys he saw every day in the projects. In school juniors and seniors were feeling him, it was just crazy.

He only had eyes for one woman, Isis. That's what he needed in a woman the traits he saw in his mother. At the rate he was going by the end of the year he would be able to show her enough money to convince her she didn't have to do any of that stuff anymore. Then he would be able to stop selling drugs. Something that he hated but felt needed to be done.

As usual school felt like it lasted forever and wouldn't wait to get home to Isis. His mother just had a way of making everything alright with a simple smile. Before his school bus stopped, he could see Baby-Ty waiting for them. Baby-Ty would always be his brother, but they chose to separate ways when it came to hustling. He wanted to ignore Baby-Ty as he waived them over, but Tanisha took off running toward him. Baby-TY wasn't only her brother he was also the only father figure she had known.

"What up lil bro?" Baby Ty could barely get the words out as Tanisha squeezed the air out of him, but he loved every second of it.

He looked at Baby-Ty with mixed emotions. Did Baby-Ty forget about hopelessness and desperation they felt that drove them to sell crack? Or was it that he was just happy to be escaping poverty? As he watched the two embrace he hoped Baby-Ty hadn't lost sight of that because if he did, he would become addicted just like the fiends they served.

"We just about to go do this homework." He answered keeping his thoughts to himself.

"You feel like taking a ride with me?" Baby-Ty asked knowing how his brother felt but also understanding why he felt that way.

Baby-Ty purple 2008 Dodge Charger, why purple Baby-Ty didn't even know, on twenty-four-inch Asantis, peanut butter leather seats that had his name stitched on the headrest in purple and two fifteens in the trunk that screamed come rob me. He had no problem being materialistic, his past gave him that right.

"Can I go?" Tanisha asked.

"Come on baby girl you know it's too dangerous for you to ride with me."

Tanisha didn't care he was always in the streets, and they rarely spent time together.

"Please Tyshaun." She begged.

Baby-TY looked at his brother for assistance.

"Sis go let Isis know we're back, I won't be long."

He agreed it was too dangerous. Now days it didn't matter if you were in the car with your family. If a nigga wanted, you they would get you.

"We won't be long I promise." He said seeing Tanisha's face sadden.

She walked away pissed of both brothers knew she'd get over it.

"Where we going?"

"Nowhere we just riding. I want to take it with my lil bro."

With all of the major cleaning out of the way Isis started on her sons mess this time. Take his shoes for example they were dirty, scuffed and wrinkled unlike other kids Isis knew her son wasn't hard on shoes. With no further thought she threw a pair of Jordans and Airforce ones. HIs clothes had a different odor to them. To her they smelled like the projects. Inside one of his pants pockets Isis came up with some wrinkled up bills. Isis always made sure he had money in his pocket what hit a nerve was the condition the money was in.

It looked as if it had switched a few hands. Isis was from the streets, so she recognized the signs when she saw them, and all began to come together. He no longer nagged when she left at night; he didn't even wait up for her anymore. It was the small things that led her to his room to investigate. She found what she was looking for in two shoe boxes, they were filled with money. Isis rubbed her temples as she felt her migraine returning. Feeling helpless she called Shaun.

"Remember that right there."

Baby-Ty was pointing out the spot where they used to hustle as he drove down a hundred thirty-fifth.

They both smiled at the memories. Baby-Ty's question didn't need an answer. They both will always remember.

"Bro stop at J&J fish."

J&J's was connected to Trogans which was on the corner of a hundred thirty fifth. The niggas from down there always posted up in front like they owned it. Baby-Ty didn't like the idea, but he was hungry, and they were already there.

"Just grab me a perch dinner... and don't be too long you know these niggas be tweaking."

He know Baby-Ty was right but the problem was he wasn't making the food. As he waited for their food which was Baby-Ty's chicken and Perch dinner, he knew Baby-Ty said perch but that's only because he thought it was the same thing. A ten-piece chicken dinner that same thing, A ten-piece chicken dinner that he and Tanisha would split and fish nuggets for Isis, he watched Baby-Ty engage a few of the dudes who were out there only the most high knew what was being said.

"Number two forty-six orders up."

"Thank you he said to the cashier handing her his ticket. She was definitely nice looking and she had some pretty white teeth. He knew because she was smiling at him.

"Ooooh.... You have some beautiful eyes." She complimented. "Ahhhhh." she screamed.

Pop! The shot was loud and clear he knew what it was. Pop! Pop! He saw the last shot go into his brother as they threw him out of his car. He ran fast as he could to his brothers side baby. Ty was laid on the pavement with his face to the sky struggling to breathe.

"Tyshawn its gone be okay bro." He dialed 911 on his iPhone.

"I told you...ugh...ugh." Baby Ty choked on his own blood.

"Shut up stupid.... so, you can breathe."

By that time, he had gotten Baby Ty head propped onto his lap. Baby-Ty began to breathe calmly.

"I'm sleepy lil bro." He barely heard him.

"No, you're not." He smacked him in hope of keeping his eyes from closing.

"Please bro don't go to sleep." He was crying now, smacking Baby-Ty harder.

"Tanisha needs you bro. I need you." He smacked harder to no avail. Baby-Ty had taken his last breath. Obviously to the crowd around him he held on to his brother his best friend.

Isis blaming herself, she wish she could have saved him

"Isis please. You have to calm down." Shaun tried to soothe her by rubbing her back. Rocking back and forth it was as if Isis didn't hear a word, he said she was unconsciously laid her head on his shoulder.

"It's all my fault. Where did I go wrong?"

"It's not your fault and it's not too late to save him." Shaun paused than continued. "You can't help him like that Isis."

Shaun was right and that's all Isis needed to hear to come back to reality. Isis roamed through the living room reminiscing on all of the pictures that went all the way back to the day she brought him home from the hospital as a newborn baby up to the present. She paid attention to every detail of every picture n hopes of finding the point where it all went wrong.

She found it. It was his twelfth birthday his smile was forced. His eyes weren't as bright, he wasn't happy.

"Oh my God." Isis cried from the migraine that just hit as reality had smacked her with a bag of bricks.

Isis massaged her temples to no avail. This was a pain no Tylenol, Advil, or Motrin could take away. Her son had changed before her eyes, and she hadn't noticed. Isis was so caught in her thoughts she barely caught him coming in. He headed straight up the stairs no hello, no hug, no nothing. It was the first time he didn't greet her, and it caused her migraine to worsen.

Good thing she didn't see what Shaun saw or it would have been the straw that broke the camel's back and sent Isis to her grave. The blood, far off look in his eyes and the zombie like state he moved in let Shaun know he'd either committed murder or witnessed a murder. Isis followed him up the stairs and almost went into shock as he lay in bed covered in blood.

"Ma, it's not my blood."

Isis continued to strip him down to his boxers. Then and only then was she satisfied that it wasn't his blood. She let out a deep breath he didn't know she was holding. But Isis could hear the pain in his voice and his eyes were lifeless. He may not have been physically hurt but something was killing her baby on the inside.

"Sweetie tell momma how you got so much blood on you."

"It's Tyshaun's ma."

He rolled onto his side away from Isis just in case a tear slipped out he never wanted his mother to see him cry. Isis was lost. How could so much of Tyshauns blood be on her son.

"He's gone ma...They killed him.... he died in my arms." He couldn't hold it anymore. The flood gates opened, and he cried a river.

Isis had never seen her son cry. He didn't even cry when he was delivered so to see made her more emotional and didn't allow what he said to register in her mind.

"I tried to save him... I swear I did but he got sleepy."

Isis was about to speak but then she understood. She felt it in her heart.

Damn near impossible only men can raise men

After his brother's death Isis couldn't tell who her eyes were open, she noticed every change.

"Isis let me help." Shaun pleaded for what seemed like the millionth time.

"No." Isis gave the same answer, "No there's nothing you can do."

"At least let me try." Shaun was determined.

At this point he was willing to do anything to get the loo of hopelessness off her face, but Isis wouldn't budge. It wasn't that she didn't want Shaun's help because she did. It would be great for her son to have a father figure it's just that Shaun would make things worse.

"I really appreciate you Shaun I do. But I can't handle this."

As she said the word's Isis didn't know if she believed them. Shaun didn't.

"Isis you've done all you could do but he's not a baby anymore. He needs a man in his life. No.... Look at me."

Isis had looked away. The truth really does hurt.

Once he got eye contact, he continued, "Only men can raise men."

"Okay."

It was a low whisper more like a sigh, but Shaun heard it. Nothing else needed to be said Shaun was on his way. "Shaun." Iris called out before he closed the door stopping him in his tracks. He hoped she wasn't changing her mind.

"Please take care of my baby."

Shaun would do just that. He just hoped that one day sooner rather than later that Iris realized her baby wasn't a baby anymore. That stopped when he sold his first bag or at least after witnessing Baby-ty get gunned down.

Shaun new the deal he'd been through it and one thing he knew was preaching didn't work. Shaun was just do his duty and give him a eighth of the game and see what he'd do with it. Realistically that was all Shaun could do.

They cruised around aimlessly in Shaun's flying spur. At first Shaun didn't know what to expect, but Iris did. He wasn't the least bit surprised to see her son take to Shaun so easily, especially with what had happened to Baby-Ty. Her only hope was that it didn't backfire because her son was far from a fool.

Shaun weaved in and out of traffic reminding him of how Baby-Ty use to drive and it always irritated the shit out of him but now it wasn't.

"What is it you want out the streets?" Shaun asked.

There was no answer, so he continued.

"Is it the money, the women, cars, clothes? What is it?"

"Man G, I don't care about that materialistic shit. My only goal is to make enough money so that Iris don't have to do whatever she does anymore." The thoughts almost made him throw up.

He never explained himself to anybody except Isis. Even more he hated talking about his mother to other people, but Shaun seemed like someone he had known forever. Even the way he gripped the steering wheel reminded him of Baby-Ty.

"I know I'm hurting her right now. I just hope one day she's able to forgive me and understand I'm doing this for her. On my b-day I'm going to stop hustling and give her all the money I have saved." It felt as if a big weight had been lifted off his chest.

Shaun was speechless. Shaun himself was a drug dealer at one point and time but he hustled because he had nothing and nobody to get it for him. Now here was somebody who had it all, but he goes it by his mother degrading herself and he wanted to stop that. Like anyone else he'd rather starve than have his mother stripping or worse to put food on the table.

"That's real shit lil bro, and I respect you for that."

It was just something about the way Shaun called him lil bro that got his undivided attention. He starred at Shaun's face and realized by why it was so familiar the eyes, the nose, the lips, even the chin. It changed everything. He now hated Shaun.

"Take me home."

Shaun didn't understand.

"Take me home now."

He was definitely pissed at something Shaun just didn't know what.

Like any other mother the only thing Isis wanted was provide for her Chile. To make sure he didn't become a product of his environment like she had. She did her best and it obviously wasn't enough. Mentally and physically, she was worn out; Emotionally she was stressed out.

Cleaning always helped Isis clear her mind and calm her nerves. So, she began to clean a already spotless house. Cleaning also helped her think. The first thought to enter Isis head was to leave the projects. They could have been moved away but no place felt safe like the projects. The thought instantly eased her migraine letting her know she was on the right track.

The door burst open, and her son flew up the stairs. It happened so quickly it left Isis with the stupid face until Shaun walked in with the same stupid face answering her question.

"I knew it." Isis said to herself following up behind her son, but Shaun heard her.

"Knew what?" He grabbed Isis by the arm before she could take another step, "Knew what?" He asked again.

Isis tried to read Shaun's face. Did he really not know?

"Do you remember Tyeisha?"

Of course, he did they were supposed to spend the rest of their lives together.

"What does she have to do with anything?" Shaun was confused. Then it hit him.

"But she said... Damn." Shaun couldn't finish the thought. He was beyond hurt.

"She lied... I watched him grow up. I watched him turn into you every day." Tears fell from Isis face not for her son but for Tyshaun. He never had a chance.

Shaun too shed tears. Deep down he knew Tyeisha was pregnant with his child, but she denied it and said the baby belonged to....

He was his own man not even him could save him

During their childhood Isis and Shaun were as close as a boy and girl could be without crossing the friendzone but there was so much they didn't know about each other. They sat on her living room sofa discussing these things. If Shaun would have had the slightest idea that Isis was pregnant, he would never have left her. He couldn't do anything for his own son, but it was possible Shaun could make it right.

He came out his room wearing all black head to toe. Which was completely different from the two-tone green Ralph Lauren Polo shirt with the matching vest and Stacy Adams to match.

"Ma, if you need me just call."

"Okay son, just don't forget to check in."

"I won't." He left without even acknowledging Shaun as if he wasn't there. Shaun wanted to say something but was stopped by the look he received from Isis.

Isis called him son instead of sweetie or baby, that kind of hurt him. But what hurt worse was it seemed like she was afraid of him, that added to the rest of his pain. Isis wasn't afraid of him. She was kind of afraid for him, there was a difference.

He had hoped the hustle of the streets would ease some of his pain. But it wouldn't. Outside the projects felt like he felt on the inside. In the projects everybody was like family. No matter the differences they may have had, what they had in common was the struggle that bond is what made them family. Baby-Ty was fami y. He wasn't one of the guys who moved to the projects or who just hung in the projects. Baby-Ty was born and raised in the projects. His death had brought tears out of known cold blooded killers. It was the first time he'd seen a grown man cry.

For the first time in his life, he could say things weren't the same in the hood. You could tell something was missing or someone for that matter. In hopes of taking his mind off it all he turned his hustler game up. Serving anybody who wanted to be served. It didn't matter if they were short or not. It wasn't about the money at the moment.

Entering the house, a strange smell hit his nose. It wasn't a stinky smell it was just different he couldn't describe it. He went to the kitchen to check if gas was coming from the stove as it does sometimes, but it wasn't.

Putting it behind him he went to check on Isis he knew he'd been driving insane. Entering her bedroom that smell hit his nose again only now it was stronger.

"Ma, you, ok?" He asked.

Her eyes were glossed but to him they looked watery.

"I will be if you watch T.V. with me." She was watching Diary of a mad black woman, a movie which was the last thing he wanted to watch but it was her favorite plus it was at the end anyway.

To his dismay Isis then wanted to watch another movie so they did. Surprisingly, he like the movie. For one all the beautiful black women kept his attention but also their stories. The feelings going on inside of him couldn't be explained. One thing that was that they were no different than his own mother and it let him know he was doing the right thing. It also made him love his mother even more. He wanted to tell her so, but she had fallen asleep. He kissed her on the cheek instead.

"This is the number one rule for your set; In order to survive you gotta learn to live with regrets..." He rapped along with Jay. Baby-Ty had every Jay album and song even if it was a feature. Knowing how Baby-Ty felt about Jay he kept his entire Jay collection. Reasonable doubt was way before his time but was just as relevant today as it was in nineteen ninety-six. Like the song "Regrets." For example.

He played the music low in hopes of not waking his mother, if she was home. He didn't want to explain why he was getting dressed at three in the morning. Checking himself out in the mirror he liked what he saw. His braids were fresh. His love mom chain glistened on his all-white Hustle Gang long sleeve with the words Hustle Gang on the front going down the sleeves with a airbrushed picture of Baby-Ty on the back with the words, Ball in paradise.

HIs Pelle jeans fit perfectly not tight but not buggy either. What he liked the most was the way his low top white and sky blue jumpmans matched his Pelle leather. It had to be like the third time his stash was short. He was a hundred percent sure he'd counted 20 bags now it was seventeen. He was tripping.

He put his faith in a .38 on his waist.

There were always guys out working the graveyard shift. In fact, some of the guys only worked the graveyard but O.G Red was one of the guys he expected to see. The second he stepped out O.G Red flicked the headlights of his twenty twelve Chevy Impala for some reason he knew the signal was for him check it out.

"The hell you doing out here, so late?" O.G. asked as he settled in.

"I couldn't sleep so I figured I'll make money before school."

It wasn't O.G. Reds place to object, but it definitely wasn't a safe time to be out.

"You to clean to be running up to cars so if you want you can work off my phone."

Everybody knew O.G. Reds phone was a gold mine. It was a no brainer for him to accept the offer. He was obvious to the fact that this was O.G. Red's way of keeping him out of harm's way. In O.G. Red's mind it was still hope for him.

He worked O.G. Red's phone until the dark sky gave way to the day. It was the easiest money he'd ever made. They would ride around the hood talking and listening to music until Reds phone rang which meant they had to meet up with a customer.

"O.G., I appreciate you spending time with me I hope this not the last time I get to pick your brain."

Red got a laugh out of that. It was refreshing nowadays lil niggas thought they knew it all.

"You're the future so there will never be a last time, that's what I'm here for." He got out the car knowing that he had someone he could always come to. That meant a lot.

"Hold on for a second," O.G. stopped him. "Take this." O.G. was referring to the thirty-eight revolver he had in his hands.

"I'm good O.G. I don't need that." His heart sped up. Guns killed people and he wasn't a killer he hated guns.

O.G. Red was having a case of Deja vu. That was the same exact response he'd gotten from Baby-Ty the night before he was killed. That answer wouldn't be accepted this time.

"It's better to have it and not need than to need it and not have it." Red placed the gun in his hand.

He watched as O.G. Red's impala turn out of the projects and thought about what he'd said and wondered if a gun would have saved Baby-Ty's life. The thought made him grip the thirty-eight tighter as if he wanted to become one with it.

"Nephew put that thing away before the police come through here."

Bridgette had brought him back to the present. "What's up auntie?" He responded as he put the gun in his Pelle Pocket never taking his hand off it. He felt powerful and he was afraid that if he let go of the gun, he would love that power.

"You working?" Bridgette asked.

He was dumfounded. He'd known Bridgette his entire life and never had the slightest idea she was a smoker. She always kept her hair and nails done. Her teeth were white, she had dark skin that was blemish free and on top of that her body was banging.

"Did you hear me? Are you working?"

"Um...yeah...yeah I'm working."

"Look out for your aunty my check comes on the first."

"If I look out for you, what are you going to do for me?"

"Anything you want me to do."

"Damn." He thought to himself.

He knew exactly what Bridgette meant but he was only talking about her making some of her spaghetti. She was famous in the hood for, but now he wanted to see what anything was. Bridgette turned around and walked away making sure to add the extra switch in her walk. He followed as if hypnotized by her hips.

He was a virgin and Bridgette was a crack head in need of her next hit and anything she could get extra. She showed no mercy on someone she looked at as a nephew as she worked for that hit. Her need for crack outweighed any moral values. As he watched Bridgette head bob up and down, he realized there was no love in the streets, all he had was himself and his thirty-eight revolver.

When you live by the gun you die by the same faith; End up dead by the age 38

"Happy birthday to you...Happy birthday to you." Isis sang to her sleeping child.

He opened his eyes and was greeted with a one-of-a-kind smile. A smile he hadn't seen in a long time, and it filled him with joy.

"Get up sleepy head."

He loved seeing her like this without that glossed overlook in her eyes. Today her dreads were pulled back putting every inch of her beautiful face on display. To Isis her son's birthday was hers as well. I represented the day she was reborn. They never did much it was all about doing it together, whatever it was. After a quick shower he returned to see Isis going through his sock drawer. He knew exactly what she would find and readied himself for the twenty-one questions.

Excuse me ma," he said reaching over her for a pair of socks.

Isis jumped as if she was the one caught in the wrong.

"Son why do you have a gun?"

"It's Tyshaun's ma I just never got rid of it." It might not have been the complete truth, but he wasn't lying.

"ISIS wiped the tears from her eyes before one could fall.

"Ma please don't cry, it's over." He begged Isis.

"Isis stop crying it's over, look," he went to the closet for the shoe boxes he had filled with money and dumped them all on the bed.

Isis was in disbelief.

"All of this for you. You don't have to strip anymore."

Hearing her son call her a stripper cut deep to her core.

"There's no more drug dealing. It's over ma, believe me. I won't hurt you anymore."

He looked Isis directly in her eyes giving her no choice but to believe him.

"Okay." It sounded like relief or defeat.

"Hurry and get dressed so we can get a move on it."

Isis turned to exit the room but stopped at the doorway.

"And son."

"Yeah ma."

"Get that gun out of my house."

Isis didn't wait on a answer but there was no way he was getting rid of his gun. The faith he once put in God was now in that gun. In his mind God failed Baby-Ty but if Baby-Ty would have had a gun he would have been alive today. What Isis didn't know wouldn't have hurt her, unless that old saying rang true.

"When you live by the gun you die by the same fate."

"Ma, can we please go now." He whined.

Isis was literally dragging him through the river oaks mall.

"We can leave as soon as you let me buy something."

He could have smacked himself he should have known that was problem.

"Okay let's go in here."

If there was anything in finish line that he wanted he, had it but it was the score they were closest to. There was nothing he wanted inside but he settled on a Chicago White Sox snap back that matched his mid-top Oreo air force ones.

"I like that White Sox snack back."

When he didn't get a response, he turned to see what his mother was up to and there was a salesman in her face laughing and smiling.

This is the main reason he didn't like shopping with her. She attracted to much attention.

"Ma, I said I like this hat, can we go now?" He rudely interrupted their conversation.

"This is cute, can we get two please?' Isis asked politely adding a smile to make up for her rude son.

"Would you like me to bag them up?"

"No." He answered.

That earned him a hour from Isis that said, "Stop it." But he shot her a look right back that said, "No you stop it."

They left finish line with their hats on backwards.

"Isis... is that you Isis?"

"What a surprise." Isis thought to herself."

By the time they made it to the Loews Movie Theater in Crestwood their movie "The Call" was already about ten minutes in but they enjoyed it. There was nothing better to the two of them than to be spending time together. They also enjoyed their time at the bowling alley. If not for all the men staring at Isis, it would have been perfect.

Isis won every game mainly because he let her, but the reason she beat him so badly was because he didn't want the gun he carried to fall out. It took a day like today to show them how they'd been neglecting each other. They were all they needed. Their ride home was silent both were in their own thoughts. Isis parked in her usual parking spot, and they say for a few minutes.

"Ma, I'm going to take a walk."

Isis knew who was on his mind therefore she didn't object even though it was late. At least she knew he'd be in the projects.

That's the life of us raised by winter, It's a cold world

Chicago winters were one of a kind. The Windy City was a nickname well deserved. It was proving that right now; the problem was it was barely thirty-seven degrees' out with a mixture of rain and snow falling from the sky. In other words, it was freezing cold.

As a hustler he loved this type of weather because it ran a lot of guys off who would otherwise be in his way of getting money. He was a winter baby, so it didn't affect him like it did everyone else. He only needed his hustle gear which consisted of two thermal tops and bottoms under a jogging suit that was under a Carhart body suit. He also wore three pair of socks inside of ACG boots.

However, today wasn't a hustler his drug dealing days were over. His White Sox hat did nothing to protect his ears. His Pelle leather was useless, and his Air Force ones felt like bricks. He had no protection from the hulk, or the freezing cold. The cold world around him didn't hurt nearly as much as thoughts of Baby-Ty.

He'd give anything to have his brother back, to feel whole again. He was so consumed in his thoughts the long walk to a hundred thirty-fifth didn't she so long. And being that his body felt just as numb as his

heart it didn't seem as cold either.

Old girl turned to coke, tried to smoke her pain

away

After framing the pictures they'd taken earlier Isis took a hot shower. After words on her way to her bedroom Isis was stopped by the pile of money on her sons bed. She wanted to ignore it but something deeper inside without allow her to. Something wanted to know.

It wasn't about where the money came from. The condition of the bills showed that. It wasn't even about how much it was. Isis needed to know if he was anything like his father, who for some reason she still loved. That's what drew her to the money. As she began to count the money Isis went back to the day, she told him she was pregnant...

"Who's is it." The words crushed her heart. He knows he was the only person She'd been with. She gave him her virginity.

Isis didn't know what to say all she could do was cry.

"I ain't got time for this shit." He turned to leave.

"Wait...wait.... Please don't go." Isis cried as she grabbed onto his arm.

"Man, just call me when you have it. If it's mine, I'll handle my business."

Isis couldn't believe her ears. This was the same person who'd sworn they would spend the rest of their lives together. Isis was the definition of a daddy's girl if there ever was one. It was the total opposite when it came to her mother which is why in times like this she went to her father. He always had a shoulder for her to lean or cry on.

"Daddy." Isis cried as she ran to her parents room.

He could instantly tell that something was bothering. His daughter was many things, but crybaby wasn't one of them.

"What's wrong with my baby girl." He asked wrapped an arm around her shoulder for comfort. Isis buried her face in fathers chest as she tried to muster up the courage to tell him.

"Daddy... I'm pregnant."

His chest mumbled his words, but he understood the "P" word. It was a loud slap in the face. The thought of his daughter having sex was enough to make him cringe but pregnant. He needed to throw up.

"It's okay baby. I'll have your mother set up an appointment for you to have an abortion."

He didn't give Isis a choice in the matter. At that point he didn't care about the psychological effects an abcrtion could have a fourteen-year-old girl. At this point his main concern was keeping up the image he created for his family at the church that was finally starting to pay off. Every project had that one family that thought they were better than everybody else. That was Isis mother and father especially her mother who always had her nose turned up at everybody. Now that there fourteen-year-old daughter was pregnant it proved that they weren't that much different. That holier than thou image was on the verge of being destroyed.

"I made my decision and that's that."

"I'm keeping my baby." Isis responded then stormed out her parents room straight to her own.

Isis knew the baby would make him love her more. She only needed to prove that it was his. She didn't understand that she was in love with a seventeen-year-old hod star living the fast life love wasn't on his agenda.

"Are you sure about this."

Isis had no idea her father followed her to her room.

"Yes daddy."

At that moment, all Isis wanted was for her father to comfort her in her time of need. However, he left her room without another word. That night Isis cried herself to sleep. Vomit in her throat forced Isis awake. Nauseous she barely made it to the bathroom. After throwing up in the toilet opened the medicine cabinet to get some mouthwash but it was empty.

Isis mother was a diabetic and her father had high blood pressure everything they needed for their health was kept in this cabinet. Something wasn't right and Isis knew what it was the second she stepped into her parents' bedroom. It was empty besides a bed and a dresser as if her parents had taken everything, they needed and left Isis with all the replaceable things.

If Isis and her mother loved each other it was only because they had to. Since day one Isis had been on the receiving end of her mother's jealousy and envy. She didn't like the love her husband gave to their daughter because it meant love was being taken from her. But Isis loved her father to death and by him she felt abandoned and betrayed. Then she felt felt hate.

Fourteen, pregnant, and alone. Abandoned by the two men she thought loved her unconditionally. To live in reality hurt too much and Isis needed to get away to escape the pain. She heard a 2 Pac song where he said, "I smoke a blunt to take the pain out, because if I was sober, I'd probably blow my brains out." At that Isis smoked her first blunt. Then she went to two a day, three a day. It had gotten to the point to where Isis needed to smoke to go to sleep and when she woke up.

Isis couldn't tell you what day of the week it neither did she care. She didn't care about school; she'd even forgotten she was pregnant times. Her future wasn't a thought about all of the allowance money she'd smoked up. She only cared about escaping the pain. "Aaaahhh." Isis groaned from the pain in her stomach. She had a growing baby inside of her and it was fed up with not being fed. There was nothing Isis wanted to do more at that moment then feed her baby, but the refrigerator was empty. So was the utility room where Isis just knew there would at least be some noodles or corn.

With no food in the house Isis decided to go to Crissy's snack shop. It was barely a ten-minute walk from the projects. Isis didn't know much about cars, but she knew a Benz when she saw one like the one sitting on Claire Blvd with its emergency lights blinking and blowing its horn for some reason Isis knew the horn waws for her. But she ignored it, she didn't know anyone with a Benz.

Isis ordered an Italian Combo dipped with sweet peppers, hot peppers, barbecue sauce, cheese, a bag of Doritos, and a guzzler. After that Isis was left with exactly two dollars and thirty cents to her name. She was broken and alone. Leaving the snack shop Isis saw that the Benz was still there. Isis didn't understand because there was no way that the driver didn't see the nasty looking projects across the street. This time when its horn blew Isis went to see what the problem was because there had to be a problem. As she approached the car a white man stepped out in a business suit that looked like it cost more than the entire projects. Isis stopped in her tracks.

"Is everything ok sir?"

The man approached Isis handing her a business card. She wasn't scared but definitely uncomfortable. The card read Johnathan Smith and Associates Attorney at Law. Isis was confused.

"What am I supposed to do with this?"

"Nothing. It's just to show you how serious I am." He stared Isis down with no shame lusting at the thought of what lay underneath her baby phat track suit. Her curvy figure had him memorized.

"I don't understand. Serious about what?" Isis had no idea what he was talking about.

He handed her an envelope containing ten one hundred dollar bills it added to her confusion,

"That's just a advance. A few friends and I are having a small party and we would like for you to dance for us."

Isis knew she should have felt insulted, but she was more curious.

"There's no sex involved we only want you to dance."

Isis wanted to say no but to give back that thousand dollars would be insane. After thinking about it Isis figured one time wouldn't hurt plus she needed the money.

"No sex?" She asked.

"Not if you don't want to."

"I'll do it."

Johnathan Smith gave her a cellphone and told her to be expecting a call.

****

They had Isis brought to a Budget Motel in Alsip. She was nervous but money was her motivation. Inside the hotel room Isis was greeted by eight middle aged white men all of them looked like they were from money. But Johnathan and their stares were frightening her.

"I can't do this." She said running out the room.

"Hey, hey, hey young lady slow down."

Isis ran straight into Johnathan almost knocking him over.

"What's wrong?"

"I don't know I just can't do this." Isis answered with her head down.

"We just want you to dance that's all. Everything will be fine."

For some reason, his words were comforting.

"But I'm scared."

The little girl came out. Either he didn't notice, or he didn't care.

He laughed, "I have exactly what you need."

He took hold of Isis hand, and she allowed him to lead her back into the room. What he thought she needed was a line of coke and it definitely help kill Isis fears. What she thought would be a onetime thing would turn into a career.

Johnathan Smith had connected Isis with all of his peers and helped her build a steady clientele of rich white men. It didn't take long for offers of sex to come. Isis turned them all down which made her wanted even more. But no matter the price Isis love would only go to the one person, and they will be a happy family once the baby was born.

Isis, life just, ended on that rainy day

She had counted almost a hundred thousand dollars and still wasn't done yet. That amount of money had a million thoughts going through her head. Like how long her son had been hustling to make that kind of money. She knew guys who'd been in the streets their entire lives who hadn't made that kind of money.

The difference from her son and must street niggas was he had no habits. He didn't smoke, drink, gamble, or trick his money on pussy, The other difference was he had no responsibilities. He didn't have any bills to pay. He didn't even by his own clothes. Neither did he have kids or siblings to provide for. That's how he was able to make that kind of money.

At one time Isis thought it was funny and cute when her son use to always talk about taking care of her. She never thought about now serious he was until now. Isis didn't bother to wipe away her tears. The house phone rang. It instantly stopped Isis heart. It was just one ring, but it was just something about it. The doorbell rang and her heart began to pump again as she got herself together to answer the door. It rang again.

"I'm coming." Isis yelled hating to be rushed.

She thought about letting whoever it was wait in the cold rain and snow mixture but knowing it was most likely Tyeisha trying to beg she wouldn't. Isis had no love or respect for Tyiesha it was only that Tyiesha's daughter, and her son shared the same father that Isis felt obligated. Before she made it downstairs the bell rang again. Snatching the door open...

"I said I was..."

It wasn't Tyeisha.

"Oh, you again."

When she got the news, her boy's body could be viewed

Isis looked at detective Jones with disgust in her eyes.

"Can I help you." Isis asked, knowing there was no way her son could have gotten into trouble so quickly.

"May I come in, please?"

"Sure."

Isis stepped to the side even though she didn't know why. Isis didn't hate the police, but she didn't like detective Jones at all. She pulled her rose tighter in fear of enticing the perverted detective.

"Let me get dressed. It'll only take a second."

"No, I think it's best that you have a seat."

Isis didn't want to sit. The longer she waited meant the longer her son would have to sit in a cage. This was always the hardest part of detective Jones' job.

"Please have a seat." He repeated.

"Nooooo." Isis screamed.

"Nooo.No. No "It was all in the detectives eyes. Isis felt it when her phone rung.

After a few gut wrenching screams Isis began to calm herself. She had to get through this she sat down calmly.

"What happened to my baby?"

Before answering the detective triec to read her body language.

"He was found dead on keystone."

How Ironic Isis thought to herself.

"How, what happened?"

Jones was hesitant before answering.

"He was shot six times… Two in the chest and four to the abdominal area."

When she got the news, her boy's body could be viewed

To his amazement Isis didn't break down she just continued to sit quietly. Isis mind was still stuck on the "He was shot six times part." What evil person would shoot her baby six times? Her poor baby who never hurt a fly. Her pour baby who would give the shirt off his back without a second shot... six times.

"Do you think you could identify the body?"

It was something Isis didn't think she could do alone. She called the one person she hoped she could still count on. Shaun waited not time coming to Isis. She didn't say why she needed him but the pain in her voice indicated it was an emergency. The second he saw detective Jones it was as if time stopped. Their history was a bad one, but it wasn't important. Isis stood not to far away looking lifeless on the inside.

"Is everything okay?" Shaun asked embracing her.

"They killed my baby Shaun." Isis cried into his chest.

Shaun began to see red. He didn't see it coming so neither did Jones when he felt the solid right crash into his jaw... than aging he went straight down.

"Shaun no please." Isis continued to cry.

But Shaun was in zone as he took the detectives gun from its holster. Aiming it at Jones head. Shaun had been waiting on this moment for almost fifteen years.

"Please Shaun. The police didn't kill him…please." For a second Isis didn't know if Shaun heard her.

"Come on Shaun we have to identify his body."

Shaun finally lowered the gun.

****

Down at the city morgue, she opened the draw saw him nude.

"Are you ready?" The medical examiner wanted to be sure.

She had been doing this for a long time and still wasn't used to kids with their lives being cut short by senseless gunfire. Isis squeezed Shaun hand.

"Yes, we're ready." Shaun answered.

The medical examiner pulled back the sheet to only reveal his face. He looked so peaceful with his braids looking just as they had when Isis did them the night before. But something was missing, as Isis looked down at her only child and only seeing the face of his father.

"He had a necklace on. Where is it?" Isis found her voice; she needed that necklace.

"Uummm, we have a watch and earrings but no necklace."

That was strange but not important at the moment. Without asking Isis removed the entire sheet. She could see we=here every bullet hit her son. It was unreal as he touched each wound starting with the chest. It was as if she could feel the bullets enter her own body as she touched each one. Everything went black.

.

Her addiction grew, prescription drugs sipping brew

The bright lights awakened Isis. She looked around and everything was white. Moving, she realizec there was an IV in her arm. She was connected to a heart monitor. Isis had no idea how she ended up in a hospital.

"Finally, you're awake."

Isis looked in the direction of where the voice came from. It was Shaun. She was still confused.

"We're at Engle's hospital." Shaun answered before she could ask.

"How long have I been here?" Isis asked, rubbing her sore dry throat.

"A few days. You had a migraine then your body shut down because it couldn't take all the stress." Shaun explained as best as he could.

Isis didn't remember anything not the phone call, the visit from detective Jones, or her trip to the morgue.

"And you've been here the entire time?" Isis asked in disbelief.

"Every second and now I'm ready to go." He joked but was very serious.

The last time Shaun was at a hospital he wasn't supposed to leave alive, and his best friend didn't even make it to the hospital. Isis didn't like hospitals either, everything about them gave her a bad vibe. With a prescription for rest and Xanax Isis was permitted to leave the hospital. On the way to her building Isis was greeted by so many people expressing their sorrows. At first, she didn't understand but then she remembered. Her son was murdered. Shut down like a wild beast her migraine returned, and it felt as if her brain would explode.

The second she stepped into her home Isis took two Xanax pills. But with one look around Isis was reminded of her lost as her living room was filled with pictures of a baby from his first days to his last. Isis felt dizzy. The two pills she had taken did nothing, so she took more. Isis wanted to begin preparing her son's funeral but the pain she felt inside was unbearable. Xanax couldn't cure it. But she knew what would. During her pregnancy Isis had a bad coke habit. The love she felt for life growing inside of her was enough to make her quit going cold turkey.

However, as is the case with most recovering addicts it only takes one event for a relapse to happen. What led to Isis relapsing was the realization of losing her son to the streets. It was the only way she knew how to cope with the doubt and fear she felt. The only thing was Isis didn't go back to cocaine she upgraded to crack. When he smelled the strange odor in his house it was crack; When he saw his mother with the glossy look in her eyes it was because she was high off crack. He wasn't miscounting his drugs when he was only a few bags short it was because Isis was smoking it. He saw all the signs but never once entertained the thought that Isis, his mother, was addicted to the shit he was selling.

Going through one of her many photo albums Isis stopped at a picture of her son along with Baby-Ty and Tanisha. Everybody said her son and Baby-Ty looked like real brothers, but Isis knew it was because of Tanisha, who shared both of their looks. If only her son and Baby-Ty did share the same father, she wondered how things would be.

She slipped into a fantasy world, had herself pregnant by a different dude

After a hard days of work Shaun returned home to an upset Isis.

"Honey is everything ok?"

Shaun's mission in life was to keep the love of his life happy.

"Of course, everything is okay." Isis replaced the sad look on her face with a fake smile, but her eyes didn't lie.

"Sweetheart I can see that something is bothering you."

"What do you want for dinner?" Isis purposely ignored his question.

Shaun looked on as Isis slammed the cabinet shut after retrieving a skillet then slamming it on the stove. She was obviously frustrated. Isis walked over to the refrigerator only to have Shaun close it as she opened it,

"Isis baby. Tell me what's wrong so I can help?"

Isis knew he meant every word she could see it in his eyes and hear it in his voice. Isis thought on it and reasoned that he would find out anyway.

"I'm pregnant."

Shaun couldn't believe it.

"What...How...I...mean..."

"See I knew it, I knew it." Isis cried.

"Knew what? And why the hell are you crying?" Shaun was lost.

"I know you're going to leave me."

Shaun laughed as he pulled Isis into him, "Isis there's no way I'm ever leaving you, I love you."

Isis believed every word. She needed to. But he did mean it and he proved it through every step of her pregnancy. Isis was in labor for sixteen hours; Shaun didn't miss a second. Neither did he hesitate to jump at the opportunity to clip the umbilical cord.

"What are we going to name him?" Shaun asked as Isis held their newborn baby in her arms.

Isis shrugged her shoulders, "I never thought about it."

Shaun had.

"Name him after me."

"You don't want a blood test first?" Her insecurities were on full display.

"Hell no!" Shaun stated clearly and firmly.

When the baby came home Isis and Shaun began to have what you would call good problems. They argued over who would change the baby and if Shaun could breastfeed? They would argue over who fed the baby. Isis considered herself lucky because some men didn't step up to their responsibility and some didn't want to be bothered until the baby could talk and walk on its own and wipe its own ass. Isis was lucky, she was in love with a real man.

"Isis, Isis!" Shaun shook Isis trying to get a response, "Isis wake up before we're late."

"Huh, Shaun." Isis was groggy.

"Where's the baby?" She said before slipping back into her fantasy world.

Shaun didn't know what just happened then he noticed the empty bottle of Xanax pills, the empty beer bottles, and what he hoped was deceiving but it looked like a homemade crack pipe.

But reality bites and this was her life

The cold water shocked her body waking Isis instantly. She had no idea how she ended up in a bathtub. Then Shaun walked in with a glass of milk.

"Drink this, it should help."

Isis took a sip but didn't know what she needed help with.

"Where's the baby?" She asked.

"Isis his funeral is in a hour."

After hearing those words Isis didn't need milk to sober her up. She was now back in reality. She didn't have a family with Shaun. Her baby was dead. Someone had taken him away from her.

****

Isis soaked in the scene in front of the friendship Methodist Baptist Church and was amazed by the size of the crowd. It was everybody from drug dealers to schoolteachers. Some of the people Isis knew, some she didn't. It was unbelievable how her son had touched so many in so little time.

"Come let's go inside." Shaun pulled lightly on Isis dim. But she resisted.

She scanned the crowd going from face to face in search of the same face her son had searched for his entire life. Shaun knew who Isis was looking for and wouldn't allow her to get her hopes up. She'd been through too much already. Shaun pulled or her arm again and this time there was no resistance and she followed him up the church steps. At the top of the church steps, they were met by O.G Red who hugged Isis as though she were his own daughter. Isis loved Red he'd come through for her when she was abandoned by her parents. He pulled the strings that allowed Isis to keep the house in the projects and she would be forever grateful for that. Isis knew without a doubt if ever she needed anything Red was there for her.

"Hey old man." Isis said returning the hug.

It was obvious that he needed one as much as she did. His eyes were puffed up and Red indicating he'd been going sleepless which was a bad combination with the Hennessy smell on his breath. In the streets the good died young while the bad grew old and gray.

There was no secret as to where O.G. Red stood. Sadly, he'd got to see many go too soon and he always felt responsible like he did now

101

and for Baby-Ty and so many before him. But it wasn't his fault that lies on the feet of whoever created the illusion called The American Dream because that's all they wanted.

Many young people in the streets have stories similar to Baby-Ty's. Crackhead mother and absent father leaving grandma to do the job, but grandma is old and sick. So, somebody has to take care of grandma and the younger siblings. Like a real man Baby-Ty accepted that responsibility.

O.G. Red was fully aware of the reasons Baby-Ty had to hustle and he only tried to guide him as best as he could. However, like many young guys who grew up with nothing and started making that fast money he was corrupted by the fame. Seeking that fame and letting it go to his head got Baby-Ty killed. When they pulled in front of J.J. 's Fish the guys down there were minding their business selling whatever they had.

"Which one of you niggas gone wash my car?"

It was supposed to be a joke, but no one was laughing.

"Man, Tyshaun take that shit back to the projects." Malcolm responded.

Malcolm and Baby-Ty went to head start at cedar together when they were kids. They were friends once but as they got older, they had to choose sides. Baby-Ty lived in the old projects and Malcolm on a hundred and thirty fifth.

"My bad Malcolm I ain't on that but you can still come to the old when you ready to make some real money." Baby-Ty flashed his bankroll for emphasis.

Malcolm laughed as he waved his old friend off knowing

Baby-Ty was only joking, but he guys he were with didn't care. He was from the projects which meant he could get it.

"Aye homie why don't you gone get up out of here." Freak suggested.

Freak wasn't a killer all he wanted to do was sell some bags and spend the money on females which is how he got his name. But S.J short for Shaun Jr. was trying to live up to the name his uncle Mike had. Mike's name put the fear of God in people and that was S. J's goal. Baby-Ty saw it getting serious.

"Aight as soon as my br..."

The first bullet from S. J's forty-five cut his sentence short. The second bullet knocked the breath out of him and the third killed Baby-Ty but this time it was different. He wasn't like Baby-Ty. He had a goal and he stuck to it. He shouldn't be buried six feet.

"I'm here too big Red." Shaun jokes.

In his drunken state Red hadn't noticed Shaun. He looked at Shaun real hard then smiled. Shaun was something he did right. There was no doubt in Shaun's mind that if it weren't for Red, he'd be either rotting in prison or rotting in dirt.

After witnessing the murder of his best friend and being shot himself Shaun made it his business to get the police officer responsible. It was O.G. Red who convinced him otherwise. O.G. Red was the reason that Shaun was now a success.

"How long has it been?" O.g asked.

"Too long." Shaun really felt that.

"Yeah, I see. You're a man now."

"Only because of you." Shaun acknowledged.

"Naw it's because of you. You don't owe me shit." O.G made it clear. "Just don't forget where you came from.

Shaun would never forget. He was Old Project born and raised and if there was anything he could do to help anyone escape the struggle, he would.

****

"I still can't believe you're gone. I still go into your room thinking I'll see you looking in the mirror. The other day I missed the bus after school because I was waiting for you. Since kindergarten we walked to school and back together." Tanisha cried as she reminded. "I guess now I can tell you that when we were in sixth grade when I told you about this boy I liked. You told me to take my time when I like somebody because boys don't get caught in their feelings like girls. Well, that boy I was talking about was you. I always loved you and I always will. Share that love with Tyshaun. Ball in paradise."

There wasn't a dry eye in the funeral. Most people knew the truth but Tanisha didn't and so he died without knowing he had a sister. When it was time to view the body, many was shocked to see he wasn't wearing a suit. Instead, he was wearing the Chicago White Sox hat that they bought on his birthday. But since his was gone he wore Isis and a black hoodie that was filled with pictures.

There was one with him and Isis, another with him, Baby-Ty, and Tanisha and the third one was of all his boys from the projects posted in front of a project building. At the top of the hoodie was the word Muddvilles and going across the bottom was the word finest. Isis knew this was how her son wanted to be remembered by his guys, his family.

On the way to the Burr Oak Cemetery the procession detoured through the Old Projects and then down to a hundred and thirty fifth. Once he got to the spot where he was killed everybody let the balloons loose and watched as they blew into the air. As the casket was being lowered into the ground everyone threw flowers into the grave. Everyone except Isis.

"Go ahead you can do it." Shaun encouraged.

But he was wrong. Isis knew throwing that flower inside the grave meant it was final and she wasn't ready for that. Isis walked to the Limo. She needed to be alone. A tap on the window brought Isis out of her deep thoughts. She got herself together before stepping out. She couldn't believe the person standing in front of her. They stood in silence before he began to shed tears.

"Don't cry…. You can't cry…. You have no right to cry." Now Isis was crying as she released fifteen years of frustration at the man who by his looks, it was obvious he had spit her son out.

"I hate…. you…. I Hate…. you, I fuck ng hate you." Isis vented and he let her. "Say something." Isis slapped him, "Say something, say anything." Isis slapped him again and again.

He accepted all that he deserved until Isis was done. Then he held out a necklace for her.

"I'm sorry." He expressed.

For Isis, the world stood still. There was only one necklace like that.

"I hate you. I swear to fucking God, I hate you." Isis snatched the necklace away.

He wasn't really her husband though he called her wife

"Why do I always have to come all the way over here and you never come to my house?"

As usual they were hugged up behind her building and he was getting tired of just hugging.

"Well because your mom don't like me and your sisters hate me." Isis responded.

"Baby my mom's do like you and my sisters are jealous because they know you're going to be my wife."

It was music to her ears.

"Say that again." She just needed to hear it.

"What that my sisters are jealous?" He smiled knowing exactly what Isis meant.

"No stupid." Isis punched him playfully on his chest. Allowing him to pull her closer by the waist looking into her big brown illustrious eyes.

"You're going to be my wife."

Isis heart smiled through her eyes.

"Do you mean it? I mean really really mean it?"

"Every word."

Isis believed him. She leaned in and kissed him. It was the first time she had tasted another man's tongue.

****

The next day in school Isis wasted no time sharing the details with her best friend, Brianna. By the time their fourth period lunch began, Isis had already talked Brianna's ears off and was still going "My husband this and my husband that."

"Isis he's lying to you. Can't you see?"

Looking at Isis you would have thought Brianna had smacked her.

"But he called me his wife. He said he'd buy me a ring." Isis needed Brianna to believe.

"So, who are you trying to convince? Me or yourself?" Brianna asked taking a bite of her cookie. Brianna never ate school lunch and it instantly let Isis know what was going on.

"Oh my God you jealous because you don't have a boyfriend."

Instantly Isis knew she was in the wrong. What she didn't know is that Brianna was only speaking from experience. Trying to save Isis from the same headache.

"I can't believe you said that." Brianna whispered.

It was obvious that Isis had hurt her feelings.

"Sorry." Isis said really meaning it and Brianna knew she did. "I just want you to be happy for me."

"He's not good enough for you Isis. You know it." Brianna said standing her ground.

"But he called me his wife." Isis expressed not seeing why Brianna couldn't accept that.

It was just this night when the moon was full, and the stars were real bright and the dress was real tight

"I love the moon. It's so beautiful." sis expressed hugged up with her man as they looked up at the stars.

"Yeah, it's beautiful." He responded not really caring. "But I love you more." He kissed the back of her neck sending tingles down her spine.

Isis turned to face him.

"Do you really mean that?"

"Yeah, I mean it." He went in for a kiss, but Isis turned away exposing her neck allowing him to lick and suck on it.

Isis felt as if she was being electrocuted.

Tonight, was the night. Isis was looking good, and he needed to feel her insides. He had to turn his game up.

"Well, what do you love about me?"

"Everything. Your smart, beautiful, loving, and caring. Your eyes reveal the innocence in you that I want to protect."

He could have continued but the way Isis covered her mouth with her hands let him know he was good.

"Now get back over here."

She came like a trained animal. It was too easy.

"You know what else I love?" He asked wrapping his arms around her. She was a goner.

"What else?" She asked with big, dreamy eyes.

"This fat ass."

He grabbed two handfuls. He'd never been this aggressive with her before but now was the time. But Isis only laughed.

"I'm serious." He said and to show her how serious he was he placed her hand on his erection. She instantly snatched her hand away.

"Don't be scared." He placed her hand back on his erection but this time he held it there. Then he moved her hand slowly up and down.

Isis heartbeat began to rise. She'd never felt anything like this before. It was warm in her hands with its own heartbeat. She could even feel it growing in her hands. After a while Isis began to move her own hand and he went back to kissing her on the neck. It felt so good Isis never wanted him to stop, but he did.

"Baby when are we going to take our relationship to the next level?"

Isis knew this moment would come one day but she wasn't ready.

"I thought we would wait until we got married."

"I know baby it's just that I love you so much. Can we just do it one time?"

Isis thought on it.

"Can we just wait a little bit longer?"

He acted as if he was thinking.

"Okay baby but I can I at least just put the tip in for a little while?" He tried.

Isis thought on it some more. They were going to get married anyway and he only wanted to put the tip in. She could do that for her husband. It wouldn't hurt to do it once.

"Okay." Isis agreed.

He couldn't believe his ears. "Are you sure?"

"Yes, I'm sure."

Isis was ready to get it over with. Her father was working overtime and her mother was out playing bingo, the usual. Isis led him to her room. Once inside Isis took off her clothes and got under the covers. He wasted no time following suit, getting on top and sliding her panties to the side ready to penetrate.

"Wait. Stop."

Isis pushed him away. "Use a condom."

He definitely didn't want to hear that. He wanted to feel all of Isis. However, he went into his pants pocket to retrieve a condom. Faking as if he was putting it on. He went to penetrate again.

"Wait." Isis stopped him.

He had to hide his irritation. "What's wrong baby?"

"Will you still have love for me after this night?"

Mike was the hard head from around the way

"Now Michael, what do you want to be when you grow up?" The teacher asked.

He'd already been around the entire class and Mike knew it would be his turn eventually. But Mike didn't know how his answer would be taken. His classmates all said things like doctors, lawyers, police officers, firefighter, football player, basketball, etc.

"I don't know Mr. Washington, I never thought about it."

"Come on Michael don't be shy. We're all in class together."

There wasn't a shy bone in his body. "Well, I want to be like my role models."

"What is it that your role models do?"

"They sell dope."

Ooohs and AAAhhs filled the classroom. Mr. Washington sent Michael to the principal's office. But Mike left the school and vowed to never come back. It was useless to him anyway.

"Lil nigga what the hell you doing?" Big Sam's voice boomed.

Big Sam was a big brown nigga who resembled Suge Knight. He was the man on this side of Muddville. Keystone was his world and a hundred and thirty fifth was his universe.

"I'm just chilling." Mike answered nervously, he knew Big Sam's reputation.

"Why your lil bad ass ain't in school it's eight o'clock in the morning?" Big Sam asked.

"Fuck school. They don't understand me in school. They not showing me how to survive, fuck school."

Big Sam felt him, but his presence would make the set hot. "I feel you lil nigga but you know it's too much going on right here so you can't stay around."

Mike knew Big Sam was trying to be nice, but he got his meaning and moved around. There was nothing for Mike to do all the kids his age was in school, and he was bored to the point where he forgot and decided to go to school. He figured he'd ask Big Sam or one of the other guys to take him.

On his way to the store where Mike liked to hangout Mike was stopped by a Ford pickup truck.

"Kid are you working?"

Mike looked at the white man, he had no idea what he was saying.

"What?" Mike asked.

"I need five and hurry up so I can get out of you guys neighborhood."

Mike understood.

"I got you just give me a second."

Mike ran home got the baking soda out the refrigerator, out it in a bowl, and added water. Then put it in the microwave so it could get hard. It was just like he'd seen in the movies.

"Hurry up." The customer rushed as soon as he saw Mike.

They made their exchange, and the customer wasted no time getting out the hood. Leaving Mike with two fifty-dollar bills. He never even checked to see if it was real crack. After that school was an afterthought. Shortly after Mike made his first one hundred dollars, he made another fifty.

It was a customer in a blue thunderbird who rode up to Mike holding up three fingers. Mike had no idea how these people just assumed he was a drug dealer. All he did was walk up and down the block. He did know at this rate there would be no more hungry nights for his family and his mother wouldn't have to work two jobs. Just to barely make it. On one of his many trips down the block he saw Big Sam again!

"I thought I told yo hard head ass to go in the house." His voice sounded like thunder.

"No, you didn't." Mike responded. "Plus, I'm out here making money."

Big Sam didn't get what Mike meant until he saw a customer ride up and Mike went to serve him.

"Hold the fuck up. Who gave you some work?"

Mike had no idea what Big Sam meant. He served the customer as if he did nothing wrong. Big Sam waited for the customer to leave.

"Who you working for?"

After seeing Mike had no idea what he meant, he took the sandwich bag out of his hands. It didn't take long for Big Sam to see that it was baking soda.

"Who gave you this shit?" Big Sam snapped.

"Nobody, it's mine." Mike answered.

It was obvious to Big Sam Mike had no idea as to what he was doing.

"Who got you out here selling this shit?" Big Sam had murder on his mind. Big Sam knew firsthand what could happen to someone selling fake crack. He'd watch his own brother get his brains blew out.

They both had copped some work neither knowing it was bogus. When the first customer came through Big Sam let his brother serve him. A few hours later that same customer came back, and Big Sam's brother got in the back seat as he did the first time. Big Sam looked away for a quick second when he heard the shot gun blast, it was deafening. The car squirted off and Big Sam watched his brother he threw out the car with his face blown off. Selling dummies was a death sentence.

Mike explained it all to Big Sam how he made his first serve. Big Sam knew it was the truth. But it was a sad truth for anyone to assume this kid was a drug dealer but now Big Sam had a decision to make.

"Are you sure this is what you want to do?" Big Sam looked Mike directly into his eyes.

"Naw. This is something that I need to do."

The rest was history.

"Michael wakes up before you late for school." His mother yelled from the bathroom as she dressed for work.

Mike heard her but he was too tired from hustling all night to move and school wasn't a thought to him anymore.

"Mike please hurry and get up. I have to go to school with you because they say you haven't been going and you know I can't be late for work."

Mike opened his eyes after hearing his mother's plea. But he didn't move he laid there and took in her beauty. Her skin was light like his. She had long beautiful hair. He loved her but hated the Ihop uniform she wore. He hated the bags under her eyes that resulted from countless hours of working two jobs.

He hated the pain in her hands and on her hands, she complained about every so often. Mike knew he was doing the right thing. Why go to school and be a part of a rigged system that didn't allow his mother to get ahead even though she worked hard every day. Even though that is what the American dream promised.

Mike sat up wiping the sleep out his eyes, "Ma, I haven't been going to school."

"Boy stop playing and let's go. You know I have to be at work at nine o'clock."

"Ma I'm serious I haven't been going to school and I'm not going back."

She knew this day was coming so it wasn't a surprise, but it still hurt. Their harsh reality was the simple fact that Mike could look out his window and see drug dealers living the good life but inside his own home he saw his mother struggling to provide the bare necessities for him and his sisters even knew one day he would feel the responsibility to provide was his. She just didn't think it would be so soon. He wasn't even in high school yet.

"Okay, I'm going to work. Just make sure the girls aren't late."

She could have out up a fight, but it would have been useless. Because she still found herself choosing between which bills pay sometimes. One of the reasons she knew her son was choosing a dangerous lifestyle.

"Okay Ma, I love you."

Mike was happy she didn't fight him on this because his mind was made up. He understood the consequences and accepted them. He only wanted to provide.

"Hey big head." Mike was greeted as he entered the kitchen, by April.

Mike had two twin sisters April and May. They were minutes apart April was born at eleven fifty-eight p.m. and May was born twelve o'clock a.m. on May first.

"Hey ugly what we got to eat." Mike asked as he opened the refrigerator. The answer to his question was obvious.

"We have cereal but not enough milk for all three of us." April answered.

When they were younger Mike would sacrifice and nut eat so his sisters could but once they were old enough to realize what he is doing. They wouldn't eat unless he ate. May entered the kitchen and as usual went straight to the refrigerator and slammed it shut.

"You hungry fat girl." Mike teased as he rubbed her belly.

May wasn't fat her body was just more developed than April's.

"Yeah stupid." She smacked his hand away.

This is why Mike did what he did. He laughed at how serious he may was as pulled some money out his pocket. He gave them both five dollars.

"You got all that money give us some more." May ordered and Mike complied giving them another five.

"Now go tell speedy I said take y'all to McDonald's and then to school and I'll take care of him.

Mike knew speedy would take care of the business. He was a smoker and Mike always hooked him up. Now it was time for Mike to take care of the empty refrigerator. It would be one less stress on his mother. Mike threw some water on his face gargled some mouthwash and went to hit the block. Mike wasn't in it to be rich only to provide for his family but how Big Sam had him checking he was on his way.

In the blink of an eye Big Sam had changed Mikes life and the life of his family. He was now in a position to keep their refrigerator full and made sure his sisters had all that they needed. His mother no longer had to choose between the gas or light bill because Mike paid them. He did all he could to ease the stress from his mother who'd done so much with so little for so long. Mike felt good, and he would feel even better once he paid Big Sam the seven hundred dollars he owed and got some more work in return.

"Mike where are you going." His mother called out from her room.

Mike had barely touched the door know and his mother couldn't even see the door from her room. Sometimes he thought she was a psychic.

"I'm going to the store, ma." He answered truthfully leaving about the part about him going to re-up on clock.

"Okay just be careful. I have a bad feeling about tonight. I would tell you to stay in, but I know you'll leave when I go to work anyway."

"Alright ma." Mike held his laughter at his mother's attempt at reverse psychology.

The nights chill instantly attached Mike the moment he stepped outside sending shivers through his body. The block was usually quiet with the exception of police sirens that could be heard in the distance. He headed to Trugans with a bad feeling in his stomach. Big Sam was supposed to be there, but he wasn't in fact no was and Mike wasn't about to wait before heading home.

Mike crossed the street to go to Maxwell's Polish. As he crossed, he could hear the police sirens getting louder. As he ordered Mike could see police lights flashing off the window. A quick look over his shoulder Mike saw squad cars from Robbins, Crestwood, and Midlothian. His order couldn't have been ready soon enough and he couldn't have been happier, once he got it, he was on his way.

"Freeze, don't move." An officer yelled jumping out of his police cruiser, gun drown.

Mike stopped to analyze the scene. No one else was out but the officer couldn't be talking to him. Before Mike could take a full step, he heard the uneasy sound of guns being cocked back.

"Don't move."

Everything seemed to be going slow motion as Mike waited to feel the pain of a bullet. Mike was accused of attempting to rob the Marathon gas station in Midlothian Illinois turned into a murder. In Illinois that's a felony murder. Mike was charged because he fit the description of being five seven to six feet tall. A hundred and fifty-two pounds, and light skinned wearing a black hoodie.

An eyewitness picked Mike out the lineup simply saying; "I think that's him." Mike was the only light skinned person in the lineup and also the only person wearing a hoodie. Two weeks before his fourteenth birthday Mike was on his way to the Cook County Juvenile Detention Center AKA the Audi home.

The crime that Mikes was accused of committing was breaking news so when Mike came in, they knew what he was fighting. Everything he knew about his case they knew. He would be the talk of the jail until the next big story broke.

"Mike what's good bro?" Shaun greeted.

Mike didn't know what to make of it. He and Shaun had fought many times just because they didn't like each other, but because they were from different sets that's just how it went, Mike squared up ready for whatever.

"I ain't on that G. We leave that on the streets. In here its Muddville or nothing." Shaun gave Mike a care package consisting of all things he needed to survive and be comfortable.

Mike was taken aback.

"Good looking bro."

"Don't trip G. You from the land. In here we all we got. It's a few more guys from the hood I'll introduce you to at school.

Mike was introduced to guys from the trailer courts, new projects off the ninth. They all accepted him but, cn the streets, they wouldn't hesitate to get down on him. Mike was also introduced to guys from other south suburbs like Chicago Heights, Ford Heights, Calumet City, Riverdale, Dolton, Calumet Park, and Harvey.

Mike wasn't surprised when he was called for a visit the next day. He just didn't know how it would go. The second he entered the visiting room his mother and sisters broke down into tears. Mike wanted to join in the crying session, but he couldn't. He had to play strong even if he didn't feel strong.

The entire visit they hugged and cried. There was no doubt in any of their minds that Mike was innocent. There doubt was in the Criminal Justice system. That was on a mission to mass incarcerate black men like Mike. That was their reality. After the visit Mike went to his cell and let all the tears, he held in on the visit flow.

Over the next few weeks Shaun showed Mike how things went at the Audi home. He introduced him to some of the staff that were cool and mostly importantly other guys who were fighting serious cases. They looked out for each other because they all were in same situation. Then Shaun was approved for house arrest.

"Man G, you gone be alright. Just keep your head up." Shaun was sincere, he didn't wish jail on his worst enemy.

Mike hoped he was right. They shook up for the last time. Letting their pitchforked finger stay connected as they made strong eye contact. Letting each other know it's been real.

"Be safe out G and remember If you gone go, then go hard."

****

"Stand next to your attorney." The bailiff instructed Mike as he entered the courtroom.

He wasn't to see him mom there but to see Big Sam at her side was surprising. At the bench before the judge were three white men. Neither looked like they were there for Mike, but the bailiff directed him to the one on the far left.

"Defendant state your name for the court."

The way she looked at Mike it was obvious he was the one she was talking to.

"Michael Smith."

"Mr. Smith is in court and in custody represented by counsel, counsel state your name for the court."

"David Weiss. W-E-I-S-S."

"Counsels defendant is before the court facing felony murder charges, correct?"

"Yes, your honor but the state has already worked out a deal with the defense."

Mike looked over at the short fat cock eyes states attorney wondering what deka he's talking about."

"Mr. Weiss can you explain the deal to me?"

"Yes, your honor. In exchange for my clients guilty plea. The state has agreed to sentence him to juvenile life." The short fat states attorney nodded his head smiling just like his bald head side kick.

"Mr. Steele do you understand what's going on?"

"No."

The judge explained to him that if he plead guilty, he would receive Juvenile life and be incarcerated until his twenty first birthday.

"Now do you understand?"

He did loud and clear they were rail roading him and he wasn't going.

"Yeah, but I'm not pleading guilty for something I didn't do."

It was obvious Mikes response rubbed the judge the wrong way as she turned her attention to his attorney.

"Mr. Weiss you and your client need to take a minute."

They were led to the back bullpen area where the other detainees were being held and put into a room that was reserved for attorneys to speak to their clients. Once the door was closed Mike didn't hesitate.

"I'm not pleading guilty to something I didn't do."

"This is what your mother wants. She's afraid of the death penalty the state is threatening."

Mike would rather be dead anyway. If he couldn't take care of his family what was the purpose of living?

"Okay I'll let her know." Mr. Weiss tapped at the door to get the bailiff attention.

"Mr. Weiss."

"Yes Michael, what is it?"

"I do not know what's going on, but I did not do this."

For some reason Mr. Weiss believed him and would do all that he could to win the case.

"Mr. Weiss, I assume you and your client are now on the same page." The judge acted as if she had something better to do. Mike began to hate her as well; it was on his face.

"Yes, your honor we are. The defense would like to file a motion for discovery."

The states attorneys were surprised. They had a deal with Mr. Weiss that in return for him for convincing Mike to plead out they would allow him to get two of his clients off. It was the same swap them out routine.

Mike received an ear full of the guys the second he stepped back into the Audi home. A lot of them were mad at him. Nobody cared if he was innocent. People copped out for cases they didn't do all of the time. The point was he had light at the end of the tunnel but instead he risked it all. Felony murder was a death penalty case. The death penalty didn't scare Mike because he'd rather die than not be able to take care of those he loved. That's what was in his heart.

"Hey Ma." Mike said as he entered the visiting room hugging his mother who was doing all she could to hold back the tears.

"Where are the girls?"

"I'll bring them next time. Today we need to talk."

Mike took a deep breathe he knew what was coming, she took one also.

"I really want you to think about…"

Mike was shaking his head.

"Damn why do you always have to be so damn hardheaded? Just listen to me one time. Just once please." The tears began.

"Ma there's no way I'm leaving you for seven years. Just trust me, I'm innocent." Mike wiped his eyes.

She knew there was nothing that could be done to change his mind.

"I do trust you, but they are seeking the death penalty for you."

He didn't want to tell her that he was willing to take that chance, so he just changed the subject.

"Thank you for the books." Mike said even though he didn't even read the titles. Reading was not on his to do list.

They talked about the twins, and she let him know that face paid for his lawyer and was also helping with bills. Mike appreciates that but didn't understand why face stepped up for him like that?

****

Two years later and Mike was still in the Audi home. He didn't believe it was taking so long to prove his innocence. The hardest part about it all was watching the twins grow up. Their bodies were developing by the day and the only thing they wanted to talk about these days were boys and it was driving him crazy.

His mother continued to send books and eventually he began to read. He'd read about some of the most amazing women like Ella Baker Sojourner Truth, Harriet Tubman, Rosa Parks. He also read about Martin

133

Luther King Jr., Malcom X, Fredrick Douglas, Nat Turner, Web Dubuis, Marcus Garvey, and others. These were people he related to and if they thought this history at school he probably would have dropped out.

The enlightenment Mike received of his history changed the way he walked and talked, and his mother recognized the profound affect it had on him. At the moment Mike was reading Miseducation of The Negroe by Carter G. Woodson when an officer banged on his door.

"Mr. Steele the officer this morning forgot to give you your mail."

Mike knew that sweet voice from anywhere, he had plenty of wet dreams with her.

"Thank you, Ms. Johnson." Mike accepted the letter intentionally touching her chocolate soft hands.

Dear Michael,

I'm so sorry you have to go through something like this. I pray every night for you to come home and I want you to know I been in love with you since the day we met.

Love, your secret admirer.

Secret admirer Mike couldn't believe it. He thought about who it could be all night until he fell asleep.

****

Mikes attorney visit had him nervous. In all of his years of being locked up he'd never had a visit from his lawyer. Like most in his position he accepted the mantra no news was good news. But now he knew some news was coming, he just hoped it wasn't bad news. He was used to Mr. Weiss wearing three-piece suits but today he dressed in a plain sweater and jeans and instead of a leather brief case Mr. Weiss had a thin folder.

"First things first." Mr. Weiss began. "The juvenile life is still on the table however, now they will allow you to parole at eighteen."

Mike thought about what he just heard. That would mean that he had less than two years. It sounded good especially since he'd seen guys be sentenced to natural life and the death penalty. If it was about him, he'd take it, but it wasn't about him.

"I'm good."

"Alright were up for jury trial. Don't worry this is what I do. I just need you to look like the innocent kid that you are." Weiss made it sound easy.

"What evidence they have against me?"

"Basically, they have a video tape of the crime though it's not good it's obviously not you. And eyewitness who if he gave his description today it would fit you but not two years ago."

"What do you think?" Mike asked.

Mr. Weiss knew the case was weak. That's one of the reasons the state wanted him to convince Mike to plea out and offered to give Mr. Weiss the better end of his next two cases. However, Mr. Weiss knew this case was too easy to give away and the publicity he'd receive after beating it meant more money for him in the long run.

"Just tell your friends goodbye."

****

Trial was finally here, and Mike was scared shitless. Deep down inside he never believed that the state would take him to trial. They had to know he was innocent. Now he saw they didn't care. They would get paid no matter what the outcome would be.

"Your honor the defense just received the rest of the discovery from the state. Based on what I have just received the defense would like to enter a motion to dismiss based on insufficient evidence."

"We object your honor. The state hadn't been made aware of any motions."

Mike still hated this cockeyed fat states attorney.

"If the state had of been tendered over all discovery instead of waiting to the last minute. This would not be a problem.

"Objection is overruled, Mr. Weiss you may proceed."

"Your honor this is simple. My client was arrested at Maxwells Restaurant in Robbins, Illinois. We have the receipt from my clients order and a sworn affidavit from the cashier placing my client at this Max Wells at eleven seventeen. This murder that happened at eleven ten took place in Midlothian, Illinois. The only states witness to point out my client in a lineup said, "I think that's him." Your horor won't allow a witness to testify as to what they think. Lastly, your honor my client was thirteen of age. He can't drive even if he could. How long would it take for him to go home which is all the way in Robbins change his clothes, then go to the restaurant. It's impossible to do that in seven minutes. Thank you, your honor."

The judge went back to her chambers to go over all she heard and compare it with the physical evidence. Mike could tell she didn't believe a word his lawyer said. Thirty minutes later she was back. She look pissed.

"The court sits here today in complete shock at the states intention of trying to take away young man's life. Your failure to investigate is sickening. You will never practice law again. Mr. Steele you can go home. Motion granted; case dismissed."

That she wanted all her life, she wanted all the hype.

Every Tuesday, Thursday, and Saturday the Flea Market came out. The Flea Market was simply a Swamp O Rama without the building or signs. Being across the alley from the projects was a lifesaver for many. It had whatever you needed when you needed it. It was where they met. He was light skinned with hazel eyes. He had a low hair cut with a braided tail in the back. He was with his mother and two sisters, who Isis dint doubt were twins.

Isis couldn't take her eyes off of him, it was love at first sight. Isis was so caught up she wasn't paying attention to where she was walking and ended up tripping over a rock and falling to the ground. Isis cried, not because she fell but because he saw it. She was embarrassed. His sisters laughed but he didn't. In fact, he came to Isis aid helping her off the ground.

"Are you ok?"

Isis couldn't respond it felt as if he would carry her off into the sunset.

"Stop being rude and tell this nice young man thank you."

Isis had forgotten she was with her mother.

"Thank you." She looked down still embarrassed.

"You're welcome beautiful."

After that, no other man had a chance with Isis she was in love. Every night she wrote in her diary about this love. Every day the Flea Market came Isis would go only to see him however, he never showed up. Isis began to accept the fact that she may never see him again. But then it happened. Isis and Brianna along with a few of their other friends were out jumping rope when he drove through the projects on his bike with his friends at least eight of them.

Isis couldn't believe it. She wanted to say something, but she couldn't, he saw her too. She knew it when he waved at her then popped a wheelie on his bike. He had Isis undivided attention even as she left the projects.

"Isis, Isis, Isis." Brianna was yelling trying to get Isis attention. "Isis!" She yelled again.

"Dang girl why you yelling in my ear like you crazy?"

"Because you stopped turning in the middle of my turn and I want to start over."

Brianna was pissed but Isis didn't realize she stopped turning.

"Sorry." Isis apologized. All the while wondering when she would see him again.

Since Isis was a little girl, her father always told her that black was beautiful, but she never believed him. Growing up she'd been called the worst names because of her dark skin and big eyes. But it seemed like overnight the teasing turned into compliments as her body began to mature. Now instead of crying herself to sleep at night from the mean things people said about her she smiled at the good things they said about her.

Like now as she wrote in her diary about her trip to the store when a sixteen-year-old boy tried to talk to her and not believing she was only thirteen or he just didn't believe her.

"Isis Brianna's here." Her brother yelled.

Isis could hear the footsteps as she hurried to put her diary away.

"Come on Isis we're going to the rink."

The Markham skating rink was the place to be for teenagers on a Saturday night.

"Right now?" Isis asked.

"Yea stupid right now, let's go."

The Markham skating rink had a skating rink inside however, many people didn't go to skate. They went to dance. The music was loud and bending vibrations throughout their bodies. It was hot and sweaty, but they loved it. Isis even more since the guys seemed to not get enough of her. She was tired but she loved dancing even more.

"Isis lets go get something to drink." Brianna screamed over the loud music.

Knowing she could use a drink Isis followed behind Brianna trying to stay close as possible. It was so crowded that with a blink of the eye they could lose sight of each other. Isis focused on Brianna but not anyone else and in the rink, you had to be on point as everyone was going every which way. It led her directly into another girl.

"I'm sorry." Isis said over the loud music she was so embarrassed.

"It's okay." The girl kept it moving.

At the last-minute Isis thought that she had known the girl from somewhere.

"Oops I'm sorry." Isis said after bumping into another girl, who smiled and continued moving.

Isis was either seeing double or she was tripping. She was a hundred percent sure that this was the same girl she'd bumped into only two seconds ago. She definitely needed something to drink.

The rink closed at eleven o clock, Isis had so much fun she couldn't wait to come back again. Outside the streets were crowded with cars. Even the parking lot to the liquor store next door was crowded as the crowd of kids tried to find their ride home. Isis was searching for Brianna's mother car when she spotted them, she knew she wasn't tripping. They were twins and Isis instantly remembered where she remembered them from. Usually, shy Isis would not let that stop her from this one in a lifetime opportunity.

"April that's the girl who bumped into me." Isis heard one of the twins say.

"Sorry about that."

They both waived Isis off as it was nothing.

"Ummm... You guys remember me?" From the looks in their eyes Isis could tell that they didn't. But she wasn't about to give up so easily.

"Okay. Well, I know your brother. I haven't seen him in a while, how is he doing?"

The twins looked at each other. Isis could tell that they were communicating something and for some reason she knew it wasn't good.

"What's wrong, is he ok?"

They could tell Isis had genuine concern, so they shared their brothers situation to her. Isis couldn't believe it. She knew he wasn't a killer; he was too nice and sweet.

She wanted all the hype

Mike went to the belly of the beast at the tender age of thirteen and was leaving out with only a few extra scars and scabs. When most would have taken the plea deal, Mike fought the system even though he knew the deck was stacked against him. His mother reminded him constantly that "A hard head made a soft ass." But this time she was wrong. A hard head didnt make him soft, a hard head made Mike a boss.

He proved everybody wrong. By now it was common knowledge who committed the crime Mike was accused of. As always, the streets talked. The streets thought that Mike would talk but he didn't fold, he kept his mouth closed. Now he was leaving South Hamilton in a limo paid for by the streets. He was on his way to Super Stardom.

The crowd in front of his house had Mike in awe. He did a three-hundred-and-sixty-degree turn observing the only hood he had known. Everything was the same, but it all seemed so different. Standing out amongst it all was his mother, his beautiful mother. Her eyes that were now filling up with tears showed that she was still in a state of belief. Now words needed to be spoken he knew what she needed, and he gave it to her with no hesitation. They hugged as if it were their first and last one. It seemed like eternity before the first words were spoken.

145

"I told you I was coming home." Mike held onto his mother as his shirt sucked up her tears.

"I know ma, I know." Mike wiped the tears from her eyes.

"Your sisters don't know your home yet. Go see them."

Mike noticed the slight change in his mother's mood. He knew the reason. On his way to his sister's room, Mike was greeted by all the guys. He didn't understand why but all of them gave him money. While the guys greeted him with handshakes and money. The females greeted him with hugs, some with more than hugs. It was odd to Mike because many of them watched him grow from a baby. But like any kid Mike had plenty of fantasies about his babysitters. By the way Mike was being felt up and complimented on his physique Mike knew those fantasies could come a reality.

Inside the house everyone was vibing to a new cat out of Brooklyn named Jay-Z. He had a laid-back flow that Mike liked. It was street music but not gangsta. It was just different from what Mike was used to. It was a first-person narrative of his life and Mike could relate to that. Many people rapped about selling drugs and most importantly how they felt as they were in the midst of selling drugs. When he rapped you could feel his fear, the doubt he had, and the hopelessness he once felt

146

along with the desperation. Most importantly he felt like the world owed him something. Mike felt the same way, the streets owed him.

"Aye lil Mike." Big Sam yelled over the loud music.

Mike had already peeped him in the kitchen area talking to slim. He was gone slide over there after seeing the twins but now that Big Sam was waving him over, Mike went to pay respects to the only father he knew.

"What's good pops?" Mike greeted. "I was gone get at you after I saw the twins." He explained.

Mike didn't acknowledge slim. Mike didn't like shit about slim. He didn't like how tall he was, his yellow skin, or that bitch ass smile he kept on his face. Slim was always in Mike's way. Slim was jealous of Mike because he too was Big Sam's protégé but now he'd grew into his own, Slim's name was ringing through the jails. He was doing his thing shining in the streets while Mike was doing time for the murder he committed.

"What's good lil homie?" Slim greeted holding his hand out for a shake. Showing that smile Mike hated.

Mike didn't want to shake Slim's hand, but Mike knew to deny Slim would be the ultimate disrespect, so he shook up with him.

"Shit just happy to be out." Mike answered while staring at the thick gold chain around Slim's neck.

"I see you been out here doing you." Mike felt like that chain should be his, the animosity could be heard in his voice.

"Go check on your sisters when you come out front, we got something for you." Big Sam interrupted.

The door to his sisters room was locked so Mike tapped lightly.

"Go away."

Mike knocked again this time a little harder.

"I said go away."

Mike could tell that it was April. He knocked even harder this time.

The door swung open.

"Are you dead…"

April was stuck. Her eyes were looking at her brother, but her mind took a little longer to register.

"Aaaahhhh." April screamed excitedly into her brothers arms. April's loud scream brought May out.

"May why are you so loud?" She asked and once May realized it she had the same reaction that April had. Now they both were Squeezing the life out of him. But Mike loved it.

"Why you didn't tell us that you were coming home?" April asked.

"Because I wanted to surprise ya'll." Mike answered however, the truth was he didn't know if he would ever come home.

"You look grown, and you got muscles and stuff." May said.

"Aye Mike." Big Sam yelled over the music.

Mike had forgotten about meeting them out front. Mike couldn't believe what they had waiting for him outside. A two-door royal blue regal on some eighteen-inch blocks.

"Aye lil nigga." Slim called out.

As soon as Mike looked back Slim threw him the thick gold chain that he was wearing. Mike was in disbelief. He looked at Slim who was on a black Suzuri motorcycle not knowing what to say.

"Welcome home lil nigga." Slim said before taking off into the night.

Mike watched him disappear and at that moment he wanted a motorcycle. He wanted everything he had to offer. The streets owed him.

"Don't just stand there lil nigga check the ride out." Said Big Sam.

The inside looked just as clean as the outside. The suede seats matched the paint job. It had a complete Kenwood Stereo System and Mike's favorite was his name stitched in the head rest.

"Come on ya'll let's go for a ride."

Mike didn't have a license, but he's driven plenty of times before getting locked up. Driving was like riding a bike. Once you had it, you had it or so Mike thought.

"Let me holla at you real quick before you leave." Big Sam said looking at April and May letting Mike know it wasn't for them to hear.

Mike knew exactly what Big Sam was asking. For Mike it was a no brainer. While locked up Mike had run across plenty who promised to change their lives some even turned to religion. Mike wasn't one of them.

"You already know what it is."

"Aight get at me when you ready and don't forget Face should be sliding on you."

Mike knew face was the other person who ran into the gas station with Slim and Mike knew Face's mcney was long. Before driving off Mike caught a glimpse of his mother peeking out her bedroom window. Worry was all over her face and in her eyes. He figured she was being overprotective and as always ignored her intuition. Some things never changed.

A new whip in the hood always stuck out like a sore thumb and Mike loved the attention he received as he cruised around the hood with his sisters. Every block Mike drove down people were trying to look through the tinted windows in hopes of getting a glimpse of who it was behind the wheel. Mike was more focused on taking in the streets he'd missed for the past couple years. Streets that would belong to him.

Mike had promised himself that if he didn't have the entire Muddville on lock by the time he was eighteen he'd give it all up. It wouldn't be right if Mike didn't slide threw the Old Projects to pay respect to Shaun. Whatever Slim had in the trunk was banging to death getting everybody's attention before he even turned into the projects.

Mike drove through slowly watching as niggas and females pointed his car out. The projects were live as always. Mike saw a dice game going on by the side of the projects and on the other side they were pitching quarters. Mike wasn't too worried about the attention his car received because while the Old Projects was known for many things robbery wasn't one of the. Mike could see Shaun anywhere and he kept driving through.

"Hey Shaun." Both his sisters screamed out the window as if he was R. Kelly or somebody.

Mike spotted him sitting on a Cutlass Supreme, Shaun knew it dint look like much at the moment, but he had big plans for it come summertime. Shaun definitely liked what he saw as the Regal was parking next to him. It didn't make him jealous it only motivated him to do better. Just as Shaun did Tyeisha heard his name being called as well. She was giving him a earful. Calling whoever the females were, every name in the book until Mike stepped out than she got quiet.

"Damn nigga. You gone show me some love or just look stupid."

Shaun hopped off his Chevy still somewhat surprised to see Mike who he'd thought he would never see outside of jail.

"You said you was gone beat the people." Shaun replied feeling as if he had beat the murder himself.

As the two talked on a crowd began to form around them. A lot of the shorties in the projects knew Mike from the Audi home so most of the conversation was about who went home, who got cracked, and who got sent to the county on automatic transfer.

"Aight you niggas be cool down here. I'm bout to ride out." Mike said not wanting to wear out his welcome.

"Same to you, my nigga."

The two embraced for what neither of them knew would be the last time. Somehow Mike had caught eye contact with Tyiesha. No words were needed. Just like everything else in the world Mike felt like Tyiesha should be his. While Mike and Tyiesha were conversing with their eyes Shaun was able to see who it was who had called his name.

"Mike folks how you know the twins?"

"Shit nigga those my sisters. How you know them?" Mike got defensive.

"Awe naw I know them from the rink. You know how it go when we leave the hood we stick together." Shaun tried to clean it up.

In reality the twins were no different than any other females in the hood. They did their dirt in other hoods where they thought niggas didn't talk too much but niggas were foul everywhere.

****

Isis couldn't believe she missed him everyone was talking about how fine Mike was, how fly his car was, the gold chain he wore, Deven Tyeisha was talking about him, and everybody knew she was stuck up and conceited. Isis couldn't help but wonder how they would talk about her once she became his girl?

She use to hold on tight when he wheelied on the bike

Unlike any other business the streets weren't supply and demand it was demand and you'll be supplied. So, what Mike did was simple he put word out that he had a half ounce o⁼ crack for whoever found a motorcycle for him. In the hood Boosters came a dime a dozen which is how he got the Helmet gloves and Jacket at a major discount.

Early Saturday morning Mike received a page from April which meant he had some new shit in. All was the clothes man he had all the hottest gear Pelle, Kar Kani, Iceberg. You name it. Ali sold clothes all over but on Saturday's he liked coming to the Flea Market across from the projects. Ali knew there was nothing a drug dealer liked more than being seen in the latest gear.

Mike knew the Flea Market would be packed but he brought his motorcycle anyway. Parking it at the exit closest to Ali hoping he didn't have to fuck somebody up. For messing with his bike. Ali eyes brightened the moment he saw Mike. He knew it meant money.

"Just the man I wanted to see." Ali said waiving Mike to the back of his red van where he kept all the good shit. "Yea man this the new shit

I was telling you about." Ali was referring to the Karl Kani jean and jacket outfits he'd pulled out the.

They all came with matching sweaters and hats. But Mike's attention was somewhere else. He was watching his bike when he saw her. Her dark skin glistened off the morning sun. She was that deep dark chocolate that Mike loved. She had big, beautiful eyes that reminded Mike of somebody.

Isis tried to avoid the Flea Market as much as possible. It always made her sad. However, today she didn't have choice when her mother sent Isis to buy the much-needed cleaning supplies like Pine Sol, bleach, dish detergent, washing powder, sos pads, etc. The lady who sold these cleaning supplies didn't hesitate to give discounts if you spent a certain amount of money. Which meant she ran out of supplies fast and she only came on the first and the third Saturday of the month.

"Baby girl let me help you with those bags." Isis rolled her eyes and kept walking. She didn't bother to turn around if a boy wanted her attention, he needed a better pick up line than that.

"Damn shorty it's like that?"

Isis continued on; she wasn't nobody shorty. She had become use to these instances from her experience the name calling would start any moment.

"Lil momma, I just want to give you a hand."

This time Isis felt him take hold of one of the bags. He had crossed the line and Isis was about to tell him so when she turned around, but she couldn't believe who she was looking at.

"Oh my God it's you." The look of disbelief shown in her eyes.

"Yeah, it's me. Now can I help you with these bags?" Mike responded not knowing who he was supposed to be.

"I wrote you." Isis didn't know what else to say.

"Wrote me?" Mike said but it was more to himself as he thought about it than it clicked. "I know you he said remembering when Isis fell. He couldn't believe that little girl had turned out to be the girl that stood before him. "You're my secret admirer?" Mike asked almost certain that she was seeing her dark cheeks turn purple, Mike was even more sure. "So does this mean you want to be my girlfriend?"

"Yeah… I mean I don't care. Isis answered and it wasn't good enough for Mike.

"Alright let me take my bike over to Ali and I'll help you take these bags home."

"Can you take me for a ride?" She had never ridden a motorcycle before.

"Yeah, let's go."

Mike gave her his helmet and jacket just in case something went wrong, He'd never taken anybody for a ride before.

"Hold on to me."

The roar of the motorcycle engine made Isis hold on tighter as Mike drove off slowly. The more comfortable Isis became the faster Mike went. He rode around the projects using the alleys in hopes of not running into the wrong people one being Tyiesha who had become a major headache. He was also avoiding the main streets because he knew his skills wasn't up to part.

"Do a wheelie." Isis asked excitedly.

Mike ignored her. Every time he had tried to pop a wheelie he'd fallen.

"Don't be scared." She challenged.

Putting his pride to the side like any man Mike would do anything to maintain his pride and without a second thought he went for it.

"Do it again, do it again." Isis was even more excited. Instilling a confidence in Mike that he'd never had before.

Without fear she had put her life in his hands. To Mike that meant she was someone special. Something loyal and trustworthy. Someone he could love.

He was a wheelie all her lifer

When Mike started hustling it was only to provide for his family. He didn't want his family to have to depend on first of the month food stamps just to eat a real home cooked meal. He wanted to put an end to the constant worry his mother had over which bills to pay and what bills to not pay. That's what he did.

He tried his best to ease the load off his mother who was living proof that the American Dream wasn't for all Americans because she worked hard every day, the evidence was all on her hands and swollen feet, but she still couldn't get ahead. The reason he loved Big Sam is because he gave Mike the opportunity to do what needed to be done.

It all went bad when mike caught his case, and he wasn't able to do what he knew was his obligation which was provide for those he loved. He thanked God for the people like Big Sam and Face who stepped up for him while he was down. Mike would never forget the night he was released from jail. He was welcomed home like a war veteran returning from battle.

Ironically, he was just like so many others who were caught up in a war. It was called the war on drugs also known as the war on black people and every night he laid in that cell he felt like a prisoner if that war. He felt like a fallen soldier. Everybody showed him love but nobody showed him love like Face.

He'd just made it in from a crazy night and couldn't wait to get some much-needed rest, but it seemed like as soon as he closed his eyes Face was banging on his bedroom window. Face was in a rush not giving Mike anytime to get himself together. Face had a lowkey Cutlass Sierra. It looked like nothing a big-time drug dealer would drive. Face didn't say where they were going and Mike followed the code of the streets, don't ask don't tell. They rode in silence until Face crosse da hundred thirty ninth going over the Kedzie Bridge.

"Don't nobody know about this spot. Not Big Sam. Not Slim, nobody."

Mike dint answer what was understood didn't need to be explained. Face turned into an apartment complex right before a hundred forty seventh.

"Make sure it stays that way." He spoke.

Face got out the car with no more words. Mike didn't know what to expect or why was Face trusting him with something he didn't trust his day one niggas with. Face and Big Sam literally came from the Mud together. Mike kept quiet and followed Face to a second-floor studio apartment. Inside the apartment there was a bed and T.V. in the only room and in the kitchen, there was only a fold out table with a few chairs around it. It was obvious nobody lived there.

Face had disappeared and reappeared so quickly Mike didn't notice. They sat at the table; it was quiet. Mike didn't want to be the one to break the silence of they eye contact. He could feel Face trying to read him.

"You ready to get money?" Face asked.

Mike nodded his head staring intently at the work Face had sitting on the table.

"What's your goal? What is it that you want out of the streets?"

"Everything." Mike answered.

Face could tell that Mike meant every word and that was good because he had every right to feel that way.

"You ain't gone be able to do that working under another nigga. You paid your dues already." Face explained. "These shorties out here love you. Pick a few of them and set up shop on your own block or alley."

Mike listened intently as Face spoke.

"I got all the work you need. That will never be a problem. The only thing I want in return is your undying loyalty."

After getting their understanding Face showed Mike how to turn cocaine into crack. Mike had taken heed to everything Face told him. He got his crew together and showed them nothing but love and they showed him nothing but loyalty in return. They were all young and hungry and after seeing the love the streets showed Mike, it made them more ambitious. Mike was proof that the shine wasn't only for the old niggas.

They loved Mike because he was out there with them every day and instead of sending them off to put in work. Mike motivated them to get money. And for that they'd kill for him and if need be, they would give their life for him.

He wasn't really the one to like

Mike's first night out was so amazing he still didn't know if it was all real or just a fantasy. When Face had come to pick him up, Mike had just barely gone to sleep. After leaving Shaun in the Old Projects Mike headed back home. He wanted to rest up for the long day he knew was coming. He knew he had to catch up for lost time.

As Mike parked his car, he saw Carmen leaving out of his house. Carmen used to babysit him and the twins when their mother worked late night shifts which to Mike seemed like all the time. Carmen had light brown skin that looked like it had a golden hue. Carmen had a slim build and Mike had never saw her without her nails and hair done. Mike had always thought she was some type of model. Six years older than Mike she was like his big sister and Mike loved her as if she was.

The twins didn't hesitate to jump out the car and greet Carmen with a hug. Mike could tell that Carmen had more of an impact on them than his mother did. Their entire style reflected Carmen's. Getting out of the car Mike received the same hug that his sisters received.

"Dang boy I been waiting on you all night." Carmen said.

Mike didn't respond he had an erection out of this world and there was no way Carmen didn't feel it poking her in the stomach.

"You looking grown, you got muscles and everything now." Carmen joked playfully running her hands up and down his arms.

"Naw you the one looking grown, you getting fat and stuff."

Carmen wasn't fat but who calls their sister thick.

"I know right." Carmen did a three-hundred-and-sixty-degree turn showing Mike her full body.

"I been working at McDonald's trying to save money for school, but I can't say no to those fries."

Mike knew that Carmen wanted to be a fashion designer he just didn't know how serious she was but now that he did, he'd do everything in his power to make her dreams a reality.

"I got you a coming home gift. Do you want it now or do you want to wait until tomorrow?"

"Hell, naw I want my shit now." Mike answered knowing tomorrow wasn't guaranteed.

"Okay come on it's in the house."

Carmen only lived around the alley from Mike. It wasn't even a five-minute walk.

As always, they entered from the back because it led straight to the basement and if you weren't family that's the only part of the house you go to see. Carmen's mother play.

"You already know just make yourself comfortable and I'll be down in a second."

Mike did just that. The basement was just as he remembered. Two couches one along the wall which Mike knew folded across the bed the other was vesicle to the first one cutting off the open space. There was also a T.V. and Vcr.

Carmen had taken so long Mike had fallen asleep and entered into dream land. It had Carmen standing before him in her birthdate suit.

"Do I still look fat." Carmen asked twirling around so that Mike could see every crease and curve on her body. Mike was mesmerized at the perfection that stood before him.

Carmen didn't wait for an answer as she placed both of his hands on her C-cup breast.

"What do you think." She asked.

Mike couldn't answer. The only thing he could do was lick his lips that had become dry all of a sudden.

Carmen took it a step further by unzipping his Karl Kani Jeans and pulling his erection through his boxer shorts. The size of Mike's erection didn't surprise Carmen she had been babysitting him for years and saw him naked on more than one occasion.

Mike gave no resistance as Carmen stripped him naked. She couldn't take her hands off his six pack that was making her hotter than she already was. Carmen kissed Mike as she stroked his erection causing a slight moan to escape his throat Carmen was ready. Taking control of Mike's length as she straddled him going down a little bit at a time until he buried into her stomach.

"Oh my God Mike." Carmen moaned as she grinded.

Mike breath got deeper and deeper as he watched Carmen slide up and his pole.

Carmen's inside was hot and tight. Mike felt like his member would literally explode. He'd had plenty of wet dreams but none that ever felt this real.

"Oooh Mike, you feel so good." Carmen continued to moan as she sped up her pace bringing Mike to his brink.

He gripped her waist hold her down. "Carmen." He blurted as he came inside of her. At that moment he realized it was not a dream.

****

The source had a Best of Hip Hop album and Mike had everybody vibing. Jay-Z and Foxy Brown had a cut on there that everybody wanted Mike to play over and over, and Mike understood why. Jay made it simple it was everything a street nigga wanted to say to their main girl and most importantly Foxy responded how every street nigga wanted their main to respond.

Mike wasn't where he was supposed to be, but he was on his way. He had the fly ass ride, the motorcycle and money to blow. His workers were loyal. But what Mike had going for him more than anything money could buy was that Mike had the baddest chick walking the streets. Carmen was his and everybody knew it. At the moment she was out of town, but it was known that Mike had done what nobody else in the hood could. On top of that Mike was hitting Tyeisha on the low. Which is where he was on his way to but before he could pull off, he heard.

"Mike why you keep ignoring my calls." Mike put his hands in his head and sighed with frustration. He knew that irritating voice from anywhere.

"Huh."

Mike turned down his radio as if he didn't hear what Brianna had said but in reality, he needed to think of a lie. But Brianna wasn't going.

"If you can huh, you can hear me."

Brianna twirled her neck, rolled her eyes stomped her foot and put her hand on her hip with all that black girl attitude. This was the reason, but Mike wasn't dumb enough to say so.

"Baby you tripping. I already told you my phone broke."

No sooner than Mike had lied did his prime co phone start ringing.

Brianna began to cry, "I thought you loved me."

Mike shook his head. There was nobody to blame but himself. As usual he let the wrong head do the thinking for him. It was about eleven o'clock in the morning. Mike was out washing his car when she by passed him going to his front door. The sun was reflected off her Carmel Skin and for some reason Mike thought she tasted like strawberries. As she walked her hips had their own Sway that hypnotized Mike.

"Who looking for."

"The twins. Are they here." Her voice sounded just as sweet as her skin. He could hear the nervousness. Just like all the other girls she was in love with Mike also. He's all they talked about.

"Yeah, they're inside go ahead the doors open."

Brianna went in and Mike followed right behind her.

"Oh shit. I forgot they went grocery shopping with my mom." Mike lied he didn't forget.

"Well just tell them I came boy."

"Wait. Wait. Wait."

Mike said approaching her from behind.

"Damn girl you smell good." Mike whispered in her ear while softly blowing it, causing Brianna's body to shiver.

"I have to go." Brianna responding trying to get away but only ended up grinding her butt. She felt all of Mike's hardness.

"Stay with me for a while. Let me make you feel good." By this time Mike was Kissing up and down the back of Brianna's neck.

"Please stop Brianna pleaded."

Once he did it was obvious Brianna wanted him to continue.

"Come on baby don't do me like this. I want to make you feel good and I want you to be my girl." Mike lied. But he knew it was what Brianna wanted to hear.

She didn't respond so Mike went in to kiss her. She accepted his tongue and allowed him to do everything he wanted to her body. She knew Mike could have any girl he wanted but out of all of them he wanted her.

"What's funny?" Brianna snapped bringing Mike back to the present.

"Nothing man. I don't know. I just can't do this hit no more." Mike responded.

Brianna didn't understand.

"Do what? What are you talking about?"

"I don't know whatever this shit is we got going on. It's over it has to stop."

"I thought you loved me." Brianna cried.

Now all the attention was on them.

"I lied." Mike responded.

"I hate you." Brianna screamed before Mike could react, she sprayed Mace all into his face and didn't stop until she felt that Mike was just as hurt as she was.

If only Isis had known Brianna was warning her from experience not jealousy.

It was a dude named Shaun

"Mr. Williams as much as I hate to do this, I'm going to send you home on home confinement. But remember the next time I see your face I won't hesitate to send you to another home that I know will get your act together understood."

By another home, the judge meant either St. Charles, Harrisburg of lil Joliet all Prisons for Juveniles.

"Yes, sir I understand." Shaun answered but violation or not there was no way he would be forced to stay in the same house as his mother.

Shaun's mother was not a crackhead or a dope fiend. That he could have dealt with. His mother was an alcoholic and while Shaun loved her to death the woman was possessed, and the demons would come out of her when she was drunk. Shaun would never forget the beatings she had given him. The scars on his face, arms back and legs would not allow him to.

The entire car ride home was silent just as their house had been since Shaun could remember. When his mother parked in front of their project building Shaun got out the car and went about his business. His mother said nothing to him as usual.

The best thing to happen to Shaun while he was locked up was meeting Mike. Shaun was amazed at Mikes ambition. Mike wanted it all and even more, so Mike believed he deserved it all. The thing about it was that Shaun knew that if Mike was to ever hit the streets again that he would accomplish all that and more. Shaun had never thought that big. His mindset was only to make it to the next day, but Mike had changed all of that for Shaun.

Before making any moves, it was only right that Shaun let Red know he was out. Red wasn't a father figure to Shaun. More of a cool ass uncle that Shaun was outside. Kicked out of school Shaun had nothing to do during those hours. And wanting to stay as far away from his mother as possible kept him out during the night. The day Red decided to see why, was no different.

"Lil homie come take a ride with me." Shaun paused in fear. He didn't know if Red was talking to him or not.

If the projects had a mayor, it was Red the older guys respected him and most importantly the younger guys loved him. In the streets it was rare for someone to have both.

"Yeah, you get in." Bed repeated.

Saying no wasn't an option and Shaun knew it. The leather seats in Reds Cadillac were more comfortable than Shaun own bed before driving off Red eyed Shaun's own bed. Before driving off Red eyed Shaun from the top his nappy head to the bottom of his pro winged shoes in which the right one had a big hole revealing Shaun's big toe that should have been covered by his socks but that had a hole in it also. Shaun also had a smell to him that was hard to ignore but he did as he drove off.

"What's the problem. Why are you always out and why don't you go to school." Red asked.

"Because ain't shit in school for me. School don't do shit about my momma beating me half to death. School don't show me how to survive in these streets and school don't do shit about me going to sleep hungry every night."

Red listened intently. He was already headed to subport which was the only restaurant open at this time unless seven-eleven counted as restaurant.

"Order whatever you want." Red said.

Shaun was skeptical. Nobody had ever offered him anything not even his own mother.

"Let me get two hot dogs, two hamburgers two fries and a sprite." Red ordered.

Red sat the bag of food on Shaun's lap. The aroma filled the car causing his stomach to grumble but he still didn't touch it and Red wouldn't force him to.

"Shorty you was just talking about going to sleep hungry. Now I ain't gone force you to eat but you could at least express some gratitude because at the end of the day I don't owe you shit. Neither does anyone else."

Red drove back to the projects without another word.

"Take yo lil ass in the house and if you want to make some money holla at me tomorrow."

Shaun's own mother couldn't make him seat in the house, but Shaun knew Red wasn't to be disrespected. The job Red had for Shaun was security or in other words a look out. His job was watch out for police and watch over the stashes for the drug dealers so that the crackheads wouldn't find and steal them. Some hustlers overpaid Shaun some under him and the others paid him what they thought his job was worth. Some weeks Shaun could make up to five hundred.

Red's intent was to keep Shaun out of the drug game, but he understood that the only thing on the mind of a shark was eat. So better for him to do. Red understood school wasn't for everyone. Red's plan was working well until the police raided the projects from every direction and one of the guys were out there with a sprained ankle. Shaun got his drugs and made a run for it but was caught and sent straight to the Audi home.

After letting Red know he was home. It was time for Shaun to put his plan into motion. When Shaun was locked up, he'd had almost two thousand dollars saved. He didn't spend money on anything but food so saving money was easy to a big-time drug dealer it was nothing but to Shaun it was everything. He used six hundred to cop an ounce of coke from Red. That he took to Lynn, who turned that ounce of coke into two ounces of crack.

Shaun sat Lynn's kitchen table and observed her every move. She moved like she cooking breakfast. He wouldn't continue to pay someone to do something he could do on his own. Being that cooking up was one of Lynn's hustles Shaun didn't expect her to teach him. After Lynn, Shaun went to find Turbo who was his best friend and shared the business plan with him. Turbo liked the idea and mentioned to Shaun the three dudes he'd been kicking it with while Shaun was locked up.

The five of them had two things in common; they didn't have fathers and their mothers were addicted to something. That was the easy part. Shaun knew the projects like the back of his hand. He could walk around all twenty-one buildings with his eyes closed. He knew where most the money came in at and would utilize the knowledge. He put two guys in the alley that connected Grace to Claire Blvd. to catch all the customers coming off Clair and he placed two in the back on Finley to catch those customers. Shaun would rotate back and forth. The name of the game for them was don't get caught. By the police or the guys.

Who was really the one to like, he really treated her right

while washing dishes.

"Yeah. It's nice out." Isis responded never taking her eyes off the Ren and Stampy cartoon.

"They're kids in the park don't you want to gout and play."

"No ma. I just want to watch cartoons."

Isis hadn't left the house since summer break started.

"Girl get yo black ass up and go play "

Reluctantly Isis did as she was told. Before she stepped out the door she began to cry. She knew what awaited her.

"Look everybody it's tar baby."

This taunting has been going on since Isis could remember. She got the point she was black and ugly and compared to most kids she was tall and skinny. Why did they always have to remind her. As always Isis tried to do the impossible and them. Isis was swing on the swing when three boys began to push her. They were pushing too hard, and Isis was going to high. She was scared. She cried for them to stop but they didn't.

"Stop before y'all hurt her." Shaun demanded, but they ignored him and him and continued to push.

But Shaun was a fighter in fact he'd had a fight with all three of them plenty of times. It took several tries, but he was finally able to stop the swing. Isis continued to cry, and it pissed Shaun off.

"Ya'll play too much. I bet ya'll won't do me like that."

"Shaun ain't nobody scared of you." KS said not wanting to be punched.

"KS I already beat you up." Shaun pulled up his sleeves as he approached them, but they stepped back meaning they didn't want to fight.

"That's what I thought only punks pick on girls." Shaun said to the three boys who would one day become his friends and hustle partners.

"Oooh y'all Shaun got a girlfriend." Tyeisha teased.

"Shut up Tyiesha you just mad done nobody like you."

"Don't worry about them." Shaun said to Isis.

"They just mad because you have pretty eyes, and your hair is longer than theirs."

Isis smiled. No boy had ever complimented before.

"I'm Shaun. If anybody mess with you again come and get me and I'll fight them for you."

Isis was lucky to have a friend like Shaun. Even though he had nappy hair and wore dirty clothes all the time. He was real friend who became a brother to her.

He wanted to run to the country to escape the city life

The sacrifice Shaun made when he got caught with the drugs paid off. The drugs belonged to Wick. The coolest nigga you'd ever meet. He was young and getting it. He repaid Shaun with a Chevy Caprice everything under the hood was brand new. The only thing hit needed was to be whipped up on the outside. Wick charged Shaun a thousand dollars for the car. Not because he needed the money but because he wanted Shaun to never think shit came free in life.

After buying the car from Wick Shaun finally began to feel like he had a purpose. It was the first time he could call something his own. He'd come along with from being the kid with nappy hair and holey shoes. Shaun couldn't wait until summertime he had plans for his Chevy Caprice that would have the streets talking for days.

Shaun along with his girlfriend Tyeisha and best friend Turbo sat on the hood of his car listening because if Jay-Z couldn't get through to him nobody could. Everybody on the team was getting money Turbo was the only fuck up. Shaun just loved him too much to cut him off. There entire crew was day one niggas. They started hustling together and that's how it would her when Shaun heard his name being called from the approaching vehicle.

Shaun didn't know who it was only that the voice belonged to a female and that the Regal was tight. The streets lights reflected of the night blue paint job and the rims. Shaun was impressed. He watched the car closely as it drove over the speed bump slowly wondering who was shitting on the land like this. What Shaun didn't expect was for the car to park next to him.

Tyiesha was running her mouth a mile a minute as always irking Shaun's nerve. Sometimes he didn't know why he dealt with her. It was more focused on welcoming Mike home something he thought would never happen. It was obvious that Mike was hitting the ground running. Shaun remembered all they talked about while locked up. Shaun knew Mike would have the streets talking and it was up to him to change the conversation. He did that ASAP.

Shaun had his Chevy painted Cherry red with the white top. He would be the first nigga in the hood to ride assassins. He turned heads everywhere he went. Which is why he always kept Turbo with him. Turbo kept a pistol on him and unlike Shaun wouldn't hesitate to use it. It was something that Turbo was good for.

"Bro turn the radio down. Jones bitch ass behind us." Shaun checked his rearview mirror and instantly his stomach knotted up. He had a four and a split of coke in the back seat Turbo had a pistol on him and on top of that Shaun had a shit load of warrants.

The good thing was Jones didn't turn on his police sirens because of that Shaun thought they might be cool. But Jones made every turn he made. Shaun didn't care he just wanted to make it to projects.

"Bitch ass nigga always on some bullshit." Turbo snapped.

"Jump out and run." Shaun ordered as soon as he turned into the projects.

"Hell naw bro. You know I ain't leaving you with this crooked motherfucker." Turbo hated Jones,

He still hadn't gotten over the fact what Jones had rubbed him and Shaun. Shaun charged it to the game Turbo hadn't. Shaun parked his car as quickly as he could, and they both hopped out and Jones was on them like white on rice. As Jones patted Shaun down, he paid no attention to Turbo creep up behind him. He would be dead if not for the look Shaun gave Turbo.

"What you doing with all this money." Jones asked after pulling a thick wad of bills from Shaun's packet.

"What money?" Shaun asked.

Jones pocketed the money. If wasn't the first time Shaun had been shaken down by Jones and wouldn't be lost.

"Got any drugs on you? He asked.

Shaun didn't even bother to answer. He signaled to Turbo that they are leaving.

Jones grabbed Shaun wrist.

"I have to take you in on the warrants." Jones had thrown bullshit in the game, but Shaun didn't care. When he heard the words warrant, he broke free from Jones and took off running. Turbo was right behind him.

They both knew what Jones would chase them until someone was caught but they'd gotten away plenty of times and today wouldn't be different. Shaun was running as fast as he could when he heard it. There was no mistaking the sound thick metal hitting concrete and Shaun knew exactly what that thick metal was Turbo stopped.

"No." Shaun tried to yell but couldn't find the breath get it out.

The three shots were thunderous. Shaun watched his best friend fall to the ground. Without thinking Shaun went back for him. He felt the pain. It was unbearing. Shaun blacked out before he could hear the actual shot. Shaun opened his eyes then immediately closed them. The bright lights were painful. Shaun tried to sit up, but the excruciating pain forced him back down.

"Nurse...Nurse."

Shaun heard his mother's voice but was too scared to open his eyes or move his head. The pain was too much.

He squinted and saw his mother standing over him with a wet face.

"Ma... ugh...ugh...ugh..."

He tried but his throat was to soar to speak. It felt like sandpaper.

"Ssshhhhh baby everything is giving to be alright." His mother soothed.

Shaun had received any affection from his mother. "Why now?" was the last thought he had before dozing off to sleep. Anita had a bad headache stemming from another hangover. It was nothing new she only needed a shot of her eighteen hundred proof.

After a nice swig from the bottle, she waited for the headache to subside. Her eyes were closed when she heard the gunshots, but it wasn't until a second later when she was sure that it was in fact gunshots. It sounded as if it wore right outside her wincow. Looking out her window Anita saw three people chasing officer Jones and she watched as some set his squad car to flames. In the distance she could hear three sounds fire sirens, police sirens, and ambulance sirens. Anita steeped outside to see what was going on. There was a crowd not too far away from her building and she went to check it out.

"Keep your eyes open…. keep fighting." Anita heard as she got closer.

It was obvious now that Jones had shot someone. But then Anita realized there were two bodies on the ground.

"There goes his momma."

A cold chill went down her spine at the crowd parted for her. She instantly recognized Turbo face. Before her eyes made it to the next victim Anita knew by the marks on his arm that it was her son. A screech came from the bottom of Anita's stomach that sounded like a wounded animal.

Somehow Shaun made it to Christ Hospital in Oak Lawn alive where they stabilized him as best, they could and waited for him to die. Shaun was shot in the chest with a police issued forty-five revolver it had barely missed his heart, but the damage was done. That was three months ago.

Shaun woke up in pain but not as much pain he was in the last time he'd awakened. His mother was rubbing the top his head. That love he'd never felt before outweighed the pain. But he still don't know why he was in pain or why the sudden change in his mother. A doctor entered the room along with two nurses and he realized he was in a hospital. But why? He couldn't remember anything. Then he did.

"Turbo."

It came out as scratchy as it felt. His mother's silence spoke louder than any words. The next month was living hell for Shaun he'd never been poked with so many needles in his life. All he heard was test, test, and more test until he was finally allowed to leave the hospital. For some reason Red was chosen to bring Shaun home. While Shaun loved and respected Red. His mind was already made up and killing Jones was a priority and either you were with him or against him.

In the projects Shaun received the type of love you can only receive in the projects, real love. This was his family. There was nothing like it anywhere else. Sometimes they fuss, sometimes they even fight but at the end of the day all they had was each other.

For the first time in his life Shaun was anxious to see his mother. He wanted to see her. Surprisingly, he was met with boxes he entered the house. Something to Shaun that it would be his things inside and after looking through one he saw that he was right. She was kicking him out. Shaun didn't know why but he was hurt and planned on expressing this to her.

Shaun knew she was either drunk already or on her way but when he made it to the kitchen where he knew she would be. Shaun was met by another surprise. Ms. Bennet. Ms. Bennet was Shaun's probation officer he'd been running from her since the last time he was released from jail. Now she was sitting at his kitchen table.

"Hey ma." He said nervously. Hello, Ms. Bennet."

"I'm happy to see that your, okay." Ms. Bennet responded with a smile that he could tell was genuine.

What was also genuine was the hug Shaun received from his mother. It was the first he could remember. He didn't know what to do but accept it.

"Sit down we need to talk."

Shaun was skeptical but he sat in front of his mother. It was the first time he saw how beautiful she was. His mother had hazel eyes. He'd never known that.

"Listen baby." She took the hand of Shaun's good shoulder into her own. Shaun was all ears.

"Ms. Bennett and I have been talking and we think it's best you move to Kentucky for their Jobs Corp program."

Shaun didn't respond. He didn't understand because there was no way he could survive in the world outside of the projects.

"We think it's best for you." Ms. Bennett added.

"Best for me? How do you know what's best for me?" Shaun exploded.

"Shaun just listen." Anita cried, "The streets almost killed you."

"No ma." Shaun lowered his voice. "The streets raised me the police almost killed me."

"Please think about it. There's nothing here for you."

"Sorry ma but I'm not going."

"It's either that or jail. Those are your only two options." Ms. Bennett stated.

Shaun attempted to get up so fast it felt as if his entire body was on fire and the pain was worse.

"I'm not going back to jail." He winched in pain.

Red had sat silently in the background watching everything unfold. He knew how to handle it.

"Anita let me talk to him, Shaun come ride with me."

It didn't make sense for a drug dealer to tell someone not to be a drug dealer, but Red was about to make it make sense.

"You're moving to Kentucky. I already have a place to stay set up for you and your O.G.

Shaun was speechless he'd never had anyone talk to him that way before. This was the first time he had news that his mother was moving with him.

"I can't survive without the projects, they're all I know. When I was hungry the projects fed me and when I was cold the projects kept me warm."

Red felt him one hundred percent.

"You saw the love you received when you came home. Those - people don't want to see you dead out here. Too many have done that already. This is your second chance at life. This is the second chance that Turbo didn't get. That BJ didn't get or Tip or Wayney. You know I can go on and on. It's on you to be the example. You don't have to die for the projects. You can live for them."

No more words were needed, Shaun was leaving but there was no way he could leave without telling Isis. On plenty of nights she'd sneak him in her house to escape the cold and the times she couldn't Isis would throw him food out of her bedroom window. More than anything she'd talk to him for hours throughout the night. Isis was the only person who knew exactly what Shaun was going through.

"Isis, Isis. Wake up."

Isis snored.

Shaun shooked her shoulder, "Isis." He said louder.

Isis opened her eyes through her blurry vison. She could make out Shauns voice, but she thought it was a dream.

"Get up we need to talk," Shaun said.

Then she knew it wasn't a dream. With that realization she jumped up faster than lightning.

"Aaaaa girl damn!"

"Sorry Shaun, I'm sorry but they said you wouldn't make it." Isis cried into his shoulder. If there was one person, she could count on it was Shaun and lord knows she needed him.

"You know they been saying that my whole life, but I'm still here." Shaun tried to make a joke out of it, but he wasn't. Obvious to many people who said he wouldn't make it to see the age of eighteen. Isis mother being one of them.

"Isis where are your parents?" To Shaun the house looked and felt like a Bando. It smelled like one also.

"I don't know. I woke up one morning and they were gone."

Her answer through Shaun for a loop, he thought Isis was the exception. She had two good parents obviously he was wrong.

"Fuck it. Come with me." Shaun couldn't leave his only friend by herself. "I'm moving to Kentucky."

Isis wanted to go badly, but how could she leave Mike?

"I can't go Shaun but please don't leave me. We can stay here together." Isis was crying again. "Your all I have."

"I have to go Isis if not I'll end up dead or in jail. My mom stopped drinking and she's moving with me. I have to do this for her."

"But what if my parents come back?" Isis was really thinking about Mike. He said he would marry her.

"Okay but if you ever change your mind, I won't hesitate to come back for you." Then Shaun did something he had always wanted to do. He kissed Isis.

"These are the keys to my car you can have it. There's three thousand dollars in the trunk inside the speaker box, it's all yours."

Isis wanted so badly to follow behind Shaun, but she was carrying another man's baby.

But Isis liked this Broadway life

Isis wasn't totally obvious to what went on in the projects, but she was sheltered from it all more than most. She'd heard gun shots; she'd even seen a gun before or at least she thought she did, but she'd never seen anyone get shut. She knew the guys standing in the front of the projects were drug dealers, but she didn't know exactly what a drug transaction was. To Isis a crackhead was a dirty snagged tooth person always looking for something on the ground. She was born in the projects, but she wasn't born in the streets.

Mike had exposed Isis to the street life. It was the fast life and she had fallen in love with it. Every time she was with him his friends treated him like a king and he always treated her like a queen. Every day with Mike was like a fairy tale he'd take her to places she never heard of. He brought her so many gifts Isis had to pass some on to Brianna because there was no way she could explain it all to their parents.

Mike threw money around as if it was growing on a tree in his backyard. Sometimes Isis wondered how he got all that money but not for long. She'd been teased so much that now that someone was showering her with expensive things it didn't matter. Isis loved Mike but he didn't know how much until the love was tested.

They were on their way to the Burr Oak Bowling Alley coming down to a hundred twenty seventh when Mike saw the police car in his rearview. Mike was guilty of being young black and driving a nice car. To police these three things separate was enough to stop and frisk but together they knew it meant drug dealer. Majority of the time they were wrong at least ninety percent of the time. But this time they weren't wrong. Mike had an ounce of crack on him from a customer he was supposed to serve but had taken too long and Mike knew better than to wait on anybody.

Right on cue the police car siren come on. Mike had been through this routine several times, be scared but it depended on Isis if he would make it home tonight or not. At that moment she had no clue what was happening.

"Isis put this in your panties." Mike never took his eyes off the road.

Isis looked at the white rock in Mike's hand she didn't know if he was serious.

"Hurry up." Mike said turning right pulling over in front of the high school.

Mike let out a sigh of relief after seeing one of the officers were black. Well at least he had black skin. Out the corner of his eye he could see Isis looking as if she'd swallowed a bird.

"Calm down baby. I'm not gone let shit happen to you." Mike assured her as he lowered the driver's window, turned off the radio, and placed both hands on the steering wheel. He didn't want any "accidents" to take place.

"Good afternoon officer." Mike greeted as the white officer approached.

"Do you know why you're being stopped?" The white officer ignored Mike's greeting.

"No sir I'm just taking my girl bowling."

"Bowling. You sure have a nice car. You sure you're not a drug dealer?"

"No sir I'm not a drug dealer."

"Sorry I don't believe you; I'm going to need for you and your girlfriend to step out of the car."

Isis stomach did flips as she stood outside the car. The way the policemen were looking at her, made her nervous. It was as if they knew she was holding drugs. But Mike knew different. Their eyes were filled with lust. The black officer searched the car while the white officer searched Mike.

"Now it's your turn miss."

Isis was scared. Mike could see the fear as she stared at him with those big brown eyes. It was as if she was begging for help, but Mike didn't know what to do. The officer started with her ankles and worked his way up. A long tear fell from her eyes. The officers eyes were focused on her chocolate thighs. He didn't see the punch as Mike punched down with all his might. The officer instantly went for his gun.

"Nooooo!" Isis screamed. She had flashbacks of what happened to Shaun and Turbo.

"Shut up bitch." The officer pushed Isis to the ground where she cried her eyes out.

"Get on your knees you fucking nigger."

Mike didn't budge. If he was going to die it was going to be on his feet. Mike didn't blink as he waited for the officer to pull the trigger.

"It's all clear in here." The black officer had finally finished his search. "Wow partner what's going on?"

"Just teaching this drug dealer a lesson." He was careful not to use the N word.

"Partner look around you."

Across the street from them at the gas station combined with a burger, a crowd of spectators had formed.

"Today is your lucky day." The officer whispered into Mike's ear as he upper cutted him in the stomach sending him down to his knees where the officer gave him another kick to the stomach.

"That's enough, now let's go."

As Mike drove away Isis couldn't take her eyes off of him. He defended her honor and for that she'd be forever grateful. Mike was upset at himself for putting Isis in that position anyway. He knew it was wrong.

She loved the Gucci sneakers, the red, green and whites

Pissed off was an understatement. Mike was two hours late and he knew she had an eleven-o clock curfew. They had planned to go out to dinner, but it looked like it wouldn't happen now. It was bad enough Isis couldn't spend as much time with him as she liked due to the unpredictable lifestyle he lived. She tried to be understanding but sometimes she needed to vent and the only person she could vent to was Brianna.

On her way to Brianna's, Mike finally pulled up. She got in the car slamming the door to express how upset she was. But Mike ignored it. When he didn't say anything about her slamming his door Isis knew something was wrong.

"What took you so long?" There was a itchy feeling in her throat. "What happened to your face and why are your eyes red and puffy?" Isis asked trying to hold down her cough.

The mace Brianna had sprayed him with wasn't as strong as it was earlier, but it was strong enough to make him use a wet towel to cover his nose and mouth. If it weren't for Isis, he wouldn't be in his car right now.

"I don't have time for this shit, come back when you feel like talking." Isis couldn't believe he had the nerve to ignore her after showing up late.

Isis pulled the door handle but before she could fully open it Mike pulled it back shut.

"I'm sorry baby. I just have a lot on my mind right now." Mike paused looking into those voluptuous brown eyes that somehow always made him weak.

"We can't go out to…" Before Mike could finish those same beautiful eyes turned into fire. "Please baby don't be mad at me. I promise I'll make it up to you."

Thankfully, the fire left her eyes. For some reason Mike couldn't stand it for Isis to be mad at him.

"So, I guess since we're not going out you don't need the clothes, I bought for you to wear?" Mike said playfully.

"Stop playing with me." Isis punched Mike on his arm playfully but with her heavy hands it always left a sting. Needless to say, Mike hated it.

"It's in the trunk."

Isis wasted no time. She practically ran to the trunk. Mike always got her expensive gifts.

"Mike hurry up."

He loved her impatience, even more he loved to make her happy.

"Okay but first tell me you forgive me."

"I forgive you."

"Tell me you love me."

"I love you stupid now open up the trunk."

Mike opened the trunk knowing that she indeed loved him. Instantly Isis smiled she loved the Gucci sandals, skirt, jacket, belt, and hat. Even more she loved the matching wallet.

"Thank you so much!" Isis said hugging Mike went in for a kiss only to be met with a cheek. "Stop being nasty." Isis teased.

The other females Mike messed with would do anything for the material things he got them but not Isis that's why he loved her. And she loved him because he never pressured Isis for sex. As she thought about these things Isis knew she couldn't leave. Mike would come around eventually. And they'd be a happy family. She knew he was the same loving and caring person she met at the flea market.

Hanging out the window when she first seen them fight

"It's seven o'clock on the dot. I'm in my drop top cruising the streets." Shaun did his best to imitate the singer and it worked.

"Oh my God Shaun that was beautiful." Isis yelled down from her bedroom window.

"Your turn Mike."

This would be Mike's only chance to win over Isis love, so he had to make it count. So, if Shaun would do usher than Mike would do genuine.

"Nine o'clock, nine o'clock hoe alone paging you wishing you were here."

"Oooh Mike, I love it." Isis cooed. She looked down at the two boys singing for her love not knowing what decision to make because choosing one meant she couldn't have the other, "Sorry but it's too tough for me to decide."

"No Isis you have to choose, I love you."

"He doesn't love you like I love you." Mike jumped in.

"I do love her." Shaun pushed Mike.

"I love her more." Mike pushed Shaun back.

Shaun took off his shirt and Mike followed suit. Both of their bodies were cut up from the nonstop workout they did every day. Rather it was running from the police or running up to a customer trying to make a sale. Isis watched as the shoving turned into punches. She didn't believe the two boys who could have any girl they wanted were fighting over her.

Isis woke in a puddle of her own juices that dream was that exciting.

How Ironic there would be one fight that would end up in a homicide that would alter their life

It was freezing cold and the twenty mile per hour wind made it feel even colder as the mixture of rain and snow fell from the sky. Mike's nose and ears were frozen numb. The hoodie and Pelle leather jacket didn't do him any justice. Neither did the Timbs. They looked good on his feet, but his feet felt like blocks. But he was a hustler and enduring this type of weather was a part of the job.

In the distance he could see someone walking in his direction. This would be welcomed company. Mike needed someone to talk to especially after the tongue lashing, he'd received from his mother and the twins. However, when Mike got close enough, he realized that whoever it was wasn't from down there. Usually, Mike wouldn't care he was too old to be set tripping, but he needed to take out his frustration on someone.

"Aye lil homie who you looking for?"

Mike didn't answer it was like he didn't exist as the lil dude bumped Mike as he passed him. Mike didn't think twice as he grabbed him by the jacket collar and threw him to the ground. Surprising Mike he hopped back up with a gun aimed directly at Mike's face... "Pops!!"

Mike at age thirty-two was still on the scene

Mike couldn't believe how far he'd come. He had money pouring in from all directions. He'd even served Big Sam weight a few times. Who would have thought it sixteen years ago. He hoped Big Sam was rotting in hell but Face he always thought about Face. Face taught him how to feed himself. It was fucked up how he went out.

It was time for Mike to re-up. Face told him time and time again to not bring his car to the spot because it garnered undue attention. Mike finally got the point and began to use hype rentals. It was rare that they crossed paths unless these meetings were prearranged so it was kind of a surprise to see Face's Thunderbird turning into the apartment complex. Unless Mike was tripping there were two heads in the car and that was odd because Face never let anyone know where he kept his shit. But at the end of the day, it was his shit.

Mike parked at the opposite side of the parking lot so that whoever it was in the car with Face wouldn't see him. He'd let Face go take care of his business before going in. No one had any idea that they were partners and Mike would keep it that way. Big Sam and slim got out of the car and Mike instantly knew something was foul. It was stamped when they pulled Face from the backseat of the car.

"Snake ass niggas." Mike said as they drug Face up the stairs.

Mike had love for Big Sam, but he was loyal to Face. And if you had no loyalty, you had no purpose to live. Mike needed to do something, but what? The single gunshot that ended Face's life ended Mike's thoughts.

"I can't believe this bitch ass nigga was holding like this." Big Sam said as he threw a duffel bag in the backseat,

"Me neither." Slim said doing the same.

Big Sam drove away as if he didn't just kill his day one nigga.

"Fuck we gone do with this car?" Slim asked.

"We gone leave this bitch behind the Trailer Courts." Big Sam answered.

Behind the Trailer Courts was dark and too quiet. Big Sam continued to drive down slim didn't know but he had planned on leaving him with the car. The loud band almost burst Big Sam's ear drum. For a second he thought Slim had beat him to the punch, but he was still alive.

But Slim wasn't, he was slumped over. The second loud bang did burst Big

Sam's eardrum and his life. Mike got out the car taking both duffel bags

with him. There was no looking back.

He had a son fifteen that he never saw twice

The thought that she'd run into the twins at the River Oaks mall never occurred to Isis. It's been a long time was an understatement, it's been fifteen years. But they hadn't changed much they were still their same goofy selves with personalities that could bring Joy to the angriest person.

"Hello ladies." Isis returned their greetings, "It's nice to see the two of you." Isis meant it. The twins were sweethearts it was their brother who was the problem.

"Girl who is this little cutie?" April asked all over him.

"Ooooh Isis he is handsome; I might be going to jail tonight." May jumped in.

Isis could only laugh as they put their twinning down. April ran her hands through his hair as May felt over his chest and arms.

"You so strong." May flirted.

"And you got some good hair." April added.

He didn't stand a chance. Isis smiled as she saw her son blush for the first time.

"We didn't know you had a brother." May said.

Isis knew this moment would come.

"I don't have a brother, he's my son."

As if they had some type of Psychic connection, they looked at Isis then to him, then to Isis and back to him. Isis didn't have to say anything, they knew the truth. Isis could tell that they had no idea that they had a nephew, and it was touching. Even if Mike didn't want anything to do wither son, his sisters had the right to make their own decision and Isis wouldn't take that away from them.

"Good Lord I think I'm having a heart attack."

The twins had relayed their encounter with Isis to their mother and it was painful.

"Are you sure?" She asked. Deep cown they would never make up a story like this.

"Yes ma, we're sure." April answered.

"Ma, he looks just like Mike." May added.

"Come on Ma you need to sit down." April pulled out a chair and May helped her take a seat. She looked as if she would faint at any second.

"How could he keep something like this from us?"

Neither of the twins could answer that in fact they had the same question. Then the unexpected happened. She cried and it was the first they'd seen their mom cry since Mike had gotten locked up which was the first time, they'd seen her cry. It caused a chain reaction. Mike entered the kitchen and was instantly met by the bad energy in the room. His presence always bought joy to the women in his life. If for no other reason than he made it home safely.

"Ma what's wrong? Is everything ok? Where's my nephew?" Mike hoped nothing was wrong with S. Dot. But it had to be something because on a good day his mom who was fifty-two could pass for forty, but today she looked every bit of sixty-five.

"Somebody tell me what's going on."

"Mike how could you keep my grandson away from me?"

"Ma you said that wasn't my son we had a blood test and everything, remember?" Mike hoped this wasn't a sign of Alzheimer's.

"She's not talking about Baby Ty." April had Mike more confused.

"We saw Isis in the mall today." May said.

That did nothing for Mike.

"Who the hell is Isis?" Mike didn't understand.

"You've been with that many women you can't remember?" Disgust could be heard all in his mother's voice.

"The only person who wrote you while you were locked up." May answered and Mike remembered.

"She was with her son at the mall today."

Now Mike saw what this was.

"Awe man she ly..."

His mother smacked the rest of the words out of his mouth, "I don't want to hear anything but you explaining yourself."

Sure, he saw him as an infant, but he dissed on him

"Aaaaaah." Isis screamed out from the pain. How could anything be this painful? And she was going through it all alone. None of the people who claimed to love her was there for her. But none of it mattered when she heard her crying baby. As she held her son, she knew she'd never be alone again.

Isis would never abandon him like so many had done her, and she would do anything to make sure he had the best life possible even if that meant using her body. For some reason Isis still believed that Mike would turn into the man she knew he was. She'd called him so many times, but it paid off when he finally showed up.

"Where is it." Mike spoke as if her son wasn't a human.

Isis was so happy that Mike was there that she let it slide. Plus, she knew that once Mike saw their son he would fall in love as she had. Isis led Mike to the room the baby was in,

"Ssshhh... I just put him to sleep."

Mike paid her no mind. His attention was on all the baby stuff. There was no way she could afford to pay for all of this on her own. He also recalled seeing Shaun's car in the front. Something was foul.

"You want to hold him?"

Mike took the baby out of her arms.

"Be careful please."

Mike was treating the baby as if it were a puppy. Twisting and turning it in the air,

"This ain't mine." Mike said almost literally throwing the baby back to Isis, "Like if that was my son, he would look so much different. See I'm light skinned and that boy there is dark."

"Wait...wait...wait, what did you just say?" Isis just knew she heard wrong.

"I said it ain't mine."

At that moment she began to hate him, but she still wasn't just going to let him leave so easily.

"Mike can you please wait." Isis said placing the baby in its crib.

"Look I ain't got time for this shit."

"Time for what?" Isis asked blocking his path.

"Get the fuck out my way." Mike demanded as he tried to go pass her.

Isis pushed him backward standing her ground.

"I told you I ain't got time for this shit."

"Well today you gone make time." Isis wasn't going. "You have your nerve saying this isn't your son." Isis pushed Mike toward the baby crib. She was pissed, "Look at him."

"Man, I already looked at it."

Isis smacked Mike so hard spit flew out his mouth, "Don't you ever refer to my son as it again."

Mike clinched his fist; it took all he had not to strike her.

"My entire family is light skin. Look how dark he is."

Isis couldn't believe what she heard she finally realized he wasn't worth it.

"You can leave now, please hurry up and leave."

"That's it?" His mother asked. There had to be more to the story.

"You mean to tell me you took advantage of a fourteen-year-old girl?"

Mike answered with silence.

"She's the same age as the twins. What if someone did them like that?"

" But Ma."

"Stop it with the buts. Your father said but all the time and you remind me of him more and more every day."

These words cut through Mike body. Was he anything like the man he swore to never become?

So, it's momma's baby daddy's maybe

It would be nearly impossible to find a man happier than Mike at the moment. He felt like he was born again. The birth of a son could do that to a man. Change his whole way of thinking and put everything in it's proper perspective. Mike may have lived a fucked-up life, but he would make sure that Baby-Ty didn't.

As he signed the birth certificate Mike felt as if he'd felt a newfound strength. Not only would he cherish his newborn son, but Mike would also cherish his son's mother Tyeisha. True enough Mike treated her badly. Like she was the scum of the earth. Somehow his mother got wind of his behavior toward Tyeisha and gave Mike a look that made him change his attitude, making him do right by her and their unborn child.

But the moment Tyeisha pushed his son out Mike had fallen in love with her. Tyeisha's mother was so upset about the fact that she was pregnant. She gave Tyeisha an ultimatum which was have an abortion or get out of her house. It wasn't a hard decision for Tyeisha to make. Mike was her mill ticket.

As she expected Mike allowed her to move in with him. He didn't like the thought of his son growing up in the projects anyway. Mike didn't think it would be something hard to adjust to, but he didn't expect for Tyeisha to be accepted so easily. His mother embraced her as her daughter and the twins embraced her as a sister.

Everything was so perfect at least as perfect as things could be with two babies running around. April had her son S. Dot a few weeks earlier. In the beginning Mike had doubts about Baby-Ty being his son but those doubts faded away more and more as he watched him grow next to his nephew. They flavored each other so much they could pass for twins; however, they weren't treated as such.

To this day his mother treated the twins as equals. It has been that way since they were born because she never wanted one to think she was better than the other. Or she didn't want one to think the other was better than her. But when it came to the babies it was clear she favored his nephew over his son. Mike didn't think his mother meant any harm because she she did show Baby-Ty unconditional love. Maybe he was tripping or maybe he wasn't. He didn't know until it was made clear.

The girls wanted to go out and being that his mother was already at bingo, Mike had to watch the babies. When it came to Mike that meant let them watch themselves. He was playing a game of NFL Blitz that had his undivided attention. As usual when his mother made it home both boys raced to her. It was clear that Baby-Ty made it to her first, but she passed him for S-Dot leaving Baby-Ty with his arms in the air. Mike had barely caught it out of his peripheral.

"Ma, why do you always do that?" Mike asked picking up Baby-Ty who still had his hand up.

"Do what?"

She was oblivious to what Mike was talking about. He was sure she wasn't doing it on purpose, but he still didn't like it.

"You walked by Baby-Ty to pick up Shaun up. Ma you always do that."

"Don't start with me Mike, I just miss my grand baby."

Mike was so caught off guard it took him longer to answer.

"Ma, Baby-Ty is your grandson, don't you miss him?"

If Mike wouldn't have been paying attention, he wouldn't have caught the look on his mother's face. It happened that fast.

"What is it ma? Tell me."

At that moment she realized she had slipped.

"I'm just tired Mike, leave me alone."

But Mike wasn't going at gunpoint. He followed his mother to her room, "Ma, you never lied to me please don't start now."

"Sorry son." She really was cause the last thing she wanted to do was hurt him. "You know I love Baby-Ty to death but he's not your son.

It was instant pain. He couldn't believe that she would say something like that.

"Ma, I don't understand."

Mike was making it harder and harder.

"Mike...son...Baby-Ty and Shaun are brothers. They have the same father."

Mike knew she was right they both looked like Shaun spit them out. Against his mother's wishes Mike sent Tyeisha and Baby-Ty on a one-way trip back to the projects. A few weeks later Tyeisha had called talking about she was pregnant. But Mike wouldn't be got again. Not by Tyeisha not by anyone.

It's been fifteen years him and Isis ain't speak, Mike needed to get out of the house and get some fresh air. Never in his life had he hurt his mother this way. That look in her eyes were too much, the twins looked at him with disgust. They were ashamed of him, Mike wanted to run away and never come back.

Then there was Isis, as he walked and talked about the good times they had and the not so good. She loved him when he was nothing, she didn't care what he had. It's been so long, if she was the mother of his son why didn't she try harder? She knew where he lived and had his number, yet she didn't try to contact him. She didn't even try to get him for child support. She just gave up on him. Mike knew he was bogus for how he treated her during her pregnancy, but he was just a nigga. A nigga taking out his frustration for Tyeisha on Isis.

If she had been more persistent, he would have come around eventually. He was just young and dumb. Now he wasn't so young or as dumb and planned on making things right. Mike thought about how he would do this as he walked.

Mike still out running the streets like life is a peach

Mike dumped the contents of the two book bags onto his bed. It wasn't hot but he was sweating. He was anxious. The kilo's of coke and bundles of money was enough to change his life, but it wasn't worth Face's life. The streets will mourn the life of Big Sam, Slim, and Face until these funerals after that it would be business as usual.

Mike had five guys who he trusted in the streets. Two were killed and the other was doing sixty years for a body leaving there of them. But after seeing what happened to Face could he really trust them. Only time would tell because after losing three major suppliers the streets were wide open and Mike had exactly what the streets needed. He'd come up on a fortune. Mike was on his way. This was just the beginning. Things couldn't be sweeter.

Until one day he approached this thug who had a mean mug. He had fight in him and Mike like that. But it was rules to this shit and an example needed to be set. Mike had him by the throat, he squeezed but then loosened his grip. It was something in the lil niggas eyes.

"Do I know you from somewhere?" Mike asked.

Told him to get the fuck off the strip but the boy didn't budge

He didn't bother to answer. He shoved Mikes hand away and kept it moving. Like nothing happened. Mike took this as a sign of disrespect which only added fuel to the fire from the tongue lashing, he'd received from his mother and sisters.

"Aye lil nigga." Mike grabbed him by the shoulder, "Where you fr…."

Mike lost his breathe. He didn't see when it was pulled but he was now staring down the barrel of a gun. He clearly had the drop, but the boy just paused, there was something in this man he knew he seen before. Mike was struck he literally had been caught slipping. He looked into those familiar eyes, and they told him one false move and he was a dead man.

"It's not that serious." Mike had thrown both his hands up in surrender. He was caught dead to the wrong.

Like looking in the mirror seeing himself more mature

His entire life he'd been searching. It had become a habitat for him to steady every mans face who crossed his path. He didn't know why until now. As he stared at the man before who had the perfect face. A face like his own. The face he was looking for.

Now he was stuck. Should he pull the trigger or not. The only thing he'd wanted in life was a father. It was the only thing his mother couldn't buy him. He'd cursed God for taking his father away. He cursed himself believing he was the reason his father left Isis. Many nights he felt insecure, less than and simply not good enough.

He felt love-hate, Joy, and anger. He was both happy and sad. These emotions were wrecking his brain. He wanted to squeeze the trigger so bad.

"Pops." He cried out for the first time in his life as he lowered his gun.

You know what they say about he who hesitates in warsth

"One more thing." OG Red hollered from his Impala.

He walked up to OG's Impala, "If you ever pull that gun out on anybody, I mean anybody. Don't hesitate to use it because they won't hesitate to kill you."

OG Red let his words sink in.

"Do you understand what I just said?"

"Yeah, OG I feel you."

"I don't want you to feel me. I need you to understand me."

There was a big difference in the two and in this instance the difference was between life and death.

"Yeah, OG I understand."

He who hesitates is lost

OG Red drove away believing that he did. He never knew what he saw before his picture went blank. Mike was taught if anyone pulled a gun out on him and didn't use it, to make them wish they had. Mike didn't think twice as his instincts was to go for his own gun. Six shots into his kid out of his gun. Mike didn't stop pulling the trigger until all six shots were fired.

Mike didn't feel a bit of remorse as he watched the lifeless body hot the ground. Mike knew he should have left the scene, but it was as if the gold chain that fell to the ground magnetic as it pulled Mike into it. It was a love mom chain and in place of the O there was a picture. Mike couldn't believe it; Isis was in the picture hugging his son. Mike looked down at his dead son and couldn't believe he had done the unthinkable. How could he go on in life? He couldn't. He put the thirty-eight to his head and pulled the trigger... Click!

Epilogue

"Isis look who's here." She got her attention.

Isis couldn't say she was totally surprised to see Mike show up. He was with his mother and the twins. April's son S. Dot was absent because he was locked up for the murder of his own brother, Baby-Ty. Whose grave was right next to her sons. They were always together. They would always be together.

Isis didn't know if she'd ever forgive Mike, but she did. She realized that Mike was a product of h is environment. Just as she was a product of that same environment. They all were, and their children paid the ultimate price. According to the Illinois Supreme Court Robbins, Illinois was among the top five poorest communities in the Chicago Metropolitan area. Poverty creates desperation, desperation is the vehicle that drives crime. Mike didn't create his cycle but if they were to overcome it, they needed to stick together.

The End

www.ingramcontent.com/pod-product-compliance
Lightning Source LLC
Chambersburg PA
CBHW051128020726
47501CB00005B/1406